ACCLAIM

"I am delighted by Gerry's ability to capture a depth of feeling and experience that goes beyond the carefully structured text. The stories combine to paint a portrait of someone special ... but for anyone who has known, worked, danced, or played with Gerry, this book captures an intimacy with a special person whose skills as a storyteller provide a personal link. As with any great storyteller, I read the stories, and it felt like Gerry was talking to me personally!"

— **Michael Brimm, Professor Emeritus, INSEAD**

"Gerry Leader locks in on character like Roger the Osprey locks in on his prey. Don't know Roger the Osprey? Let *Marjorie to Sophia - Thirty Years of Stories* introduce you. Along the way, you'll discover Sophia Loren at 30,000 feet, a young soldier's eye-opening experience of racist leadership, and how two become one on the dance floor. As Sophia might say with a wink: Magnifico!"

— **Paul McLean, author of** *Blood Lines*

"This powerful collection of stories presents an engaging flow of events, encounters, and self-realizations in the long and accomplished life of a remarkable man. These intimate reports, delivered in a personal and engagingly self-deprecating way, provide vivid insight to the development of a humanist educator dedicated to teaching the ways and means of developing leadership via collaboration. His uneven path to success in over nearly nine decades is readily recognizable and deeply inspiring."

— **Mike Mayo - retired Director of Development, WGBH**

"*Marjorie to Sophia* offers a mini journey from a beginning, a state of innocence to a state of wisdom, insight, growth, earned from new knowledge, a suffering, a loss, a joy, a collaboration, a love. Gerry's people, places, and cultures are real, colorful, varied, wide-ranging, visceral. To live as story, to record them, and to pass them on is a a gift. In these you have done as Ralph Waldo Emerson said: 'I do not give you my time, but I give you that which I have put my time into, namely my letter or my poem, the expression of my opinion, or better yet, an act which in solitude I have learned to do.'"

— **David Cave,**
Director of Development, MIT M6edia Lab

The last 20 odd years, Gerry has shared life and career wisdom, spousal and parenting tips, and many of the stories recounted. He is sometimes a James Bond or an Indiana Jones, sometimes a teacher and mentor who changes the arc of your life with questions and encouragement, and always a good friend with a kind sense of humor. These stories offer a deeper glimpse into one of the world's finest men and the people who made him. I will re-read this often!"

— **Anurag Banerjee**
CEO & Founder, Quilt.AI

"Gerry is a natural and gifted storyteller, transporting us from his childhood in Saint Louis, Missouri to the halls of Harvard Business school, gardens of Kyoto, and a visit with the Maasai people in Tanzania with grace and wit. These stories are a testament to a highly observant sensitivity, and a beautiful love of life."

— **Michela Moscufo, independent journalist**

MARJORIE TO SOPHIA
– THIRTY YEARS OF STORIES

GERALD C. LEADER

Publisher's Information

ISBN: 978-1-953080-56-1

Author contact: gleader@bu.edu

Cover design by Kristin Leader

© 2025 by Gerald C. Leader

EBookBakery Books

Dedicated to Storytellers Everywhere

Contents

ACKNOWLEDGMENTS

This book was sparked by real stories... those of my grandfather, Conrad Leader; my father John C. Leader; my mother Marjorie Leader; my children: Wren, Kristin, and Jody and her husband Paul McLean; my grandchildren: Asher, Jerilyn, Emily and Michela; and my wife, Lucy.

Gratitude has been on my mind of late, and what has emerged in my daydreams are memories of the men and women I encountered growing up in the late 1940s and early 1950s and throughout my adulthood. In seemingly subtle and unintentional ways, they came through for me and deserve a belated thank you from a guy to whom they unknowingly gave hope.

Many neighbors, colleagues, friends, and teachers informed the life experiences chronicled in this collection. How fortunate I am to have been the recipient of their wisdom, humor and advice. Their support has led me to the startling conclusion that I'm not the only author of my stories. A host of characters from elementary school to the present impacted my life. We crossed paths and our intersections have led to remarkable new beginnings; they helped to shape my trajectory and set me on new courses. I raise them to co-author status now because I ask myself, "What if we hadn't bumped into each other, what then?" This book is my way of honoring these life-altering mentors.

I count Jay O'Callahan as my formidable guide and storytelling coach for 30 years. His graceful, playful, intelligent, and faithful process gently guided me to write authentically. Doug Lipman also lent his talents as coach for the first couple years. Our group of 'Monsters': Carol Burnes, Joe Dinmore, Katie Green, Lyn Hoopes, Steffen Landauer, Susan Lenoe, and Pam MacFarlane, Theo Page, and Toby Page, who enhanced my creativity with their affirmations.

Editor Tracy Hart has understood the nuances of my stories and has enabled my words to better represent who I am.

I have been most fortunate to rely on the expertise of I. Michael Grossman, my publisher, to give shape to my stories.

Thanks also to Michela Moscufo for proofing the final draft.

Kristin Leader, my daughter, created the elegant cover for From *Marjorie to Sophia - Thirty Years of Stories*. I am grateful for her signature, creative graphic gifts.

My partner of 47 years, Lucy Aptekar, has had a profound effect on me. Her encouragement throughout my years of writing stories and compiling them into this book has been constant. She never gives up on me, applauding my creative energies and affirming the worthiness of these tales. I've counted on her editing skills for over 30 years to ensure that my words craft the meaning I intend. I am thankful for her in my life.

PREFACE

Thirty years ago, I was attracted by an advertisement in a journal from Jay O'Callahan, a professional storyteller. He invited people to participate in a workshop designed to increase creativity by writing and telling stories.

Following the conclusion of the 2-day introductory workshop, the 12 of us who enrolled were inspired to continue what we had experienced. We invited Jay to organize a second overnight workshop at the country retreat house of one of the members. A joyful event, it led us to plan subsequent gatherings, with Jay as our mentor and guide for 30 years.

We met twice a year for 4-day sessions, alternating at members' homes and found ourselves in utter delight - writing stories, cooking meals, and fashioning playtimes that captured our imagination. The group has weathered members moving away, Covid-19, and the realities of aging and end of life, and when meeting in person wasn't possible, we chose to gather online. We continue to meet and create stories to this day!

Marjorie to Sophia - Thirty Years of Stories owes its creation to these committed gatherings of an inspiring and talented band of merry writers. I hope these humorous, sad, inquiring, and wondrous tales pique your interest and encourage you to write your own!

BEGINNINGS

My Mother Marjorie also Told Stories...

EARLY IN SPRING, WHEN SOME mornings the frost is white in the black dirt, Papa goes out to plow. Mare, the mule, pulls the 300-pound, steel plow and Papa guides it. The ground is rough with roots and stones, but Papa makes it look easy, feathering over the rows with big, brown Mare with heavy hooves, pulling steady. Papa runs the plow down and back, down and back, and Marjorie waits at the end of the row in the clover, feeling the rumble of his plow through the ground, waits to see Papa every time he circles round so they can tell their stories.

"Ho, Mare!"

"Papa, a four-leaf clover!"

"What you going to wish, Marjorie?"

"You to stop plowin' Papa, and sit in the sun; we'll tell a story."

"What about, Marjorie?"

"Summertime. A summer story, Papa."

"We'll unhitch Mare, and ride out through summer."

Papa turns the plow. "Go, Mare!"

Mare starts down the new row, black dirt spilling out in a wide wake behind the plow and Marjorie begins the story. The words seem to come from the rumble of the ground. They float in her mind and sometimes she lets them whisper out onto the wind.

Summertime, Papa, the trees heavy and green, and shadows deep in the grass. Hot summertime, Papa, with long grass and crickets and Katydids singing and the bees yellow in the goldenrod, gathering honey, the honey flows full now, the hot, hot summer sweet now, full and sweet and hot in the deep grasses, the stonewall warm, the weeds deep, the clover full. The field rustling in corn, corn whispering in the wind as we ride along.

I sit forward, you behind, and Mare goes easy, slowly across the upper field, rocking us along on her boat-back, carrying us on her wide strong back, the rhythm of wheat in the summer with the quick song of the crickets. You above me, shoulders shading like a giant tree, riding, your arms round my arms holding the reins, easy, hands loose, riding easy.

Hot, but still early, it's early and we're out in the hot, holding the day ahead of us, all ahead, stretching out before us like the wide field, we ride. We unhitch Mare and ride above the rustling corn, shining silver, tall and thick and silver, out into the high pasture, through the deep goldenrod, through the break in the stonewall, the stand of birch, with the sunlight speckling, flickering over the ferns, tall deep ferns, and moss on the rocks, cool in the shade.

We follow the fox trail through the stand of birch, Grampa's birch, and on up the rocky blueberry hill, Mare's hooves chinking on the rock, kicking out stones, the blueberries turning, over the wild hill, covered in low, thick blueberries hot on the rocks, up over the hill on Mare, your hands easy, riding easy, our legs swinging, feet hanging easy, my hands in Mare's mane, holding easy.

"Ho, Mare!" Papa stops at the end of the row and looks down at Marjorie.

"Where'll we go, Papa?"

"The river...Go, Mare!"

Papa starts down a new row and Marjorie goes on telling him the story in her mind.

...On past the blueberry field, through the stonewall, tumbled down stones, on across the high field, high in the blue-sky field, with the swallows darting, and Mare's hooves soft in the soft grass, swallows swooping, swooping and diving across our path, singing, the daisies white in the wind, white and shining, the grasses blowing now in the wind, the wind rippling waves in the grasses, deep cresting waves, rising, falling.

Now down, down, and hear the river down below, down under the ridge, trees standing tall on the hill above the river, their trunks deep in shadow, their tops in sky. Down, Mare walks carefully down, stepping slowly. We lean back to help her, lean back not to slide down over her neck as she steps down, steep, feel the cool come up from the river, ride up on the shadows, wrap round us, smell the river, cool. Shiver. Shiver, river.

The shivering river wonders, wanders, slows, waits for us in a little pool, waits for us, stops its wandering, wondering, wandering, and wakes to find us in. We are in and the river is ready, riding us out, carrying us out into the morning, sweeping us softly into the day, away, away on the eddies, the running river, tumbling river, big bumbling river, buoys us up, sweeps us along, along the blue-black, silver, sweet silver rumbling rippling, riding, roving river, wandering, wondering, waking -- waking to find it is holding us now at last.

"Ho, Mare!" Papa stops the plow and rests on its long arm, looking down at Marjorie.

"Where's the river go, Papa?"

"Come, we'll climb the barn. You'll see..."

Papa unhitches Mare. Marjorie climbs on her big boat-back and Papa leads them up the field, Mare's hooves chinking stones, the sun freckling their shoulders, lifting the last of the frost from the yellow winter grass. At the barn, Papa lets Mare loose in the paddock.

They step into the tack room. Marjorie sinks back on the great grain sacks and breathes the dark smell of oats and molasses. Papa hangs Mare's tack on the wall and lifts his hammer down. Marjorie watches him loop it through his belt and thinks about the empty nails on the wall, nails for bridles. She wishes for a bridle of her own, a bridle and saddle, a horse of her own.

She follows Papa out of the tack room and slowly up the long wooden ladder, rung after rung, her hands grasping the rough wooden bars, her feet sure, one by one, rung after rung, after Papa. His feet, her hands, his feet, her hands, rung after rung, up over the hayloft, the darkness rich around them, the smell of dust and hay and old, cold winter close around them. Up, rung after rung, Papa's feet, Marjorie's hands, hands, feet, hands, feet, rung after rung, up toward the bit of sky bright and high at the peak of the dark roof. So very high. Marjorie holds the ladder, hand over hand, and there, a nest, where the eaves come in, close at the peak of the roof.

Papa bangs with the hammer. Bang, Bang, bangs open the little door in the cupola at the top of the eaves. Bang. Suddenly the light flashes in bright, and the smell of sunshine on the breeze blows into the dark heart of the barn. Marjorie climbs one last rung, swings through the little door, out onto the roof. Papa follows. The breeze flies up round them, early spring breeze rising up from the paddock below, smelling deeply of ground. The breeze lifts round them, and the sun in little whispers flickers in her eyes, the ground below, quiet, not talking to her now, but silent, looking away, turning its back and looking away. The sky, bright and wide, reaches around her, holding her, coming close, close around her, holding her and welcoming her into its blue, filling in, sweeping under her, silently gathering her in, holding her in its blue, blue light.

"There's the river, Marjorie…"

Papa holds Marjorie's hand and points with their two hands to the river shining through the bare trees beyond the plow, on the far side of the blueberry fields. Marjorie looks down on the field, all still to plow, and Papa's furrows, his morning plowing, bright in the spring sun, the fields rolling to the gray-trunked trees along the river, the river, a silver sliver shining, threading away down the valley.

And birds. On the wind, birds. Swallows swim up suddenly, darkening their sky, flashing their shadow on the barn roof, rippling off with a windy whir, and the sky around them wraps closer. The wind, too, comes closer. Papa holds Marjorie's hand and they listen to the sigh of the breeze, to the quiet coming up from the fields and the stillness of the hills away down the valley, the maple tops in new, soft red, listen as the wind round them, sighs, Fly...Fly...

Feet fluttering, legs like ribbons, together they fly out onto the wind, float out lightly, lift over the roof of the barn, the paddock, pasture pond, float out over Papa's plowing...and on, over the high fields, down the steep ridge to the river, out over the water swimming silver beneath them, silver and shining, wandering, wondering, dancing in eddies, whipping puffs, rippling, flowing deep, slowing, waiting in shallows, shimmering, feathering, flooding, and forgetting, nearly forgetting, but no, not ever forgetting, pulling them along on its deep river song.

"Where's the river go, Marjorie?"

"To the city, Papa ... the city, with the shiny black horses and the buggies all in a row, the big clock on the tower, and the bells..."

"What'll you do in the city, Marjorie?"

"Ride the carousel, Papa."

"What you goin' to ride?"

"The Bay...with the red blanket."

"Where you goin', Marjorie?"

"Round and round, Papa, round and round, and up and down...round ...and round...and away...we ride out over the fields, Papa. We run through the grasses. His name is Zephyr, Papa, He runs like the wind. Down by the pasture pond we stop, low out of the wind in the quiet. I take off Zephyr's saddle. The blanket is all wet, Papa. I lay it on the grass to dry. We're going bareback, Papa, but Zephyr is too high. He steps near a big rock. I pull myself up on his back, throw my leg over, wrap my arms round his neck."

"Where will you ride, Marjorie?"

"Zephyr knows, Papa. I don't hold the reins. I go where Zephyr goes."

Bang. Bang. Papa nails shut the cupola door and they climb slowly down into the dark winter heart of the barn, down the ladder, rung after rung, Papa's feet, Marjorie's hands, feet, hands, down, and out. Papa lifts Marjorie up onto Mare's big back, and they start slowly down to the field. Papa hitches the plow, and Marjorie sits at the end of the row in the clover, feeling the rumble of the ground, waiting for Papa to circle round so they can tell their stories.

CHILDHOOD MENTORS

IT'S 1941; I'M SIX YEARS old living in a lower middle-class suburb of St. Louis, and it's time for me to ride a two-wheeler. All the other kids are doing it. Mom's hesitant, but Dad knows he can teach me to ride in one go at it.

At Sears & Roebuck, he buys me their Hi Ho Silver Streak with white-walled balloon tires and horsehide tassels streaming from the handlebar grips. It was supposed to be my choice, but Dad couldn't resist the cowhide tassels plus the cowhide seat. Dad, relatively short and stocky and prematurely balding, has never ridden a two-wheeler, but he was an expert horseman, having grown up on a ranch in Idaho. Riding and training horses was a learned talent of his.

I should have known he would lead the bicycle like a horse, holding onto the handle bars and then trotting alongside as we descend steep Rupert Avenue, heading straight for Big Ben Boulevard where traffic is at its busiest. We gather speed, but Dad, panting, is still holding on. To this day, I can't say for sure, but I believe Dad twice whispers to the bike, "Whoa, Whoa…"

We sail past Mom, arms flailing, screaming, "Jack, Jack!"

I'm no help. I'm paralyzed with fright. Yesterday, Jackie Seefurd told me to peddle backwards to brake, but I haven't practiced it, and Dad hasn't mentioned it. The bike wants to outdistance Dad. But Dad, not letting this critter have the upper hand, takes the lead and crosses the boulevard. He pushes his left arm out, palms signaling traffic to STOP, and brings a Buick

Roadmaster with a lion-mouth grill to a screeching halt. The rest of the cars follow suit, making a clear path through which Dad triumphantly leads the bike and me to Wood's Ice Cream, across Big Ben Boulevard, where he treats me to a double-dipped chocolate cone. What Dad misses in bicycle acumen he more than makes up for as a model of determined bravery, which I will never forget.

Gratitude has been on my mind of late, and what has come forward in my daydreams are memories of men and women who, in subtle ways, came through for me while I was growing up in the late 1940s and early 1950s. They deserve a belated thank you from a guy whom they unknowingly gave hope.

Dad is first in line, but Mrs. Matthews, my third-grade teacher, has to be second. She was my guardian angel, always unobtrusively there when I was most in need.

It's 1:45, June 30, 1944, the day before summer vacation. Every single other kid has passed in their multiplication tables test. Nine times seven has stumped me again. I'm sweating and feel the red glow of shame spread across my face. Mrs. Matthews, surveying the classroom, meets my ready-to-cry eyes and smiles. My relief is instantaneous, even before her walk to my desk. A momentary glance at my exam and then she gives me an assuring smile. Surprisingly, I'm still at peace, even calm, when she asks me to wait while penning a note to Mom.

Maybe taking third grade over again won't be so bad. It will be easier the second time. But when Mom opens the note, she, too, smiles, not a common practice for her. If over the summer I can learn the 12 times multiplication tables with Mom's help, Mrs. Matthews will promote me to 4th grade - and I do.

Passing the three R's, while a struggle, was not my biggest worry at East Richmond Elementary School, a sturdy, red brick structure circa 1920s, three floors high. Fire drills were my true nemesis. Try as I may, when the fire bell clanged, I couldn't make myself go down the spiral slide encased in a ten-foot-wide steel cylinder. In its earliest incarnation, it must have been a grain storage silo. To access it on the third floor, a teacher pulled open a large metal portal door revealing a moldy smelling, black space which could only be the entrance to hell as my Sunday school teacher had described it.

Heights and darkness were not my friends. Other kids thought the ride down was great fun, but I imagined otherwise each time we were beckoned. I required a stiff push-start much to Principal Cheney's consternation.

"State law requires students to voluntarily enter and push themselves off," he insisted.

The fateful day when I was to jump on my own or be sent home, I couldn't stop trembling as I sat perched at the entrance. I was alone, that is, until Mrs. Matthews came over. Standing behind me, and with words of encouragement (and unnoticed by anyone else), she gave me a gentle but powerful kick in the butt that sent me careening down the slide. This she repeated at every fire drill.

At all costs, Principal Cheney was to be avoided. His physical appearance telegraphed his reputation as a stern disciplinarian: short with a bulldog physique and fiery red hair covering his arms, neck and oversized head. Being ushered into his office, as I was after recess one April morning, was particularly frightening.

I had started out the day close to euphoric with mastery of my newly-created musical instrument. I had found a quarter-sized, hollow toy-train wheel, which when placed between my front and lower teeth and blown in and out through, could make tunes. The kids at recess, particularly the girls, marveled at my virtuosity and asked where they could find such an instrument.

But when trying to answer and whistle at the same time, I swallowed the toy-train wheel!

Stunned, embarrassed, and panicked, I started for home but was intercepted by the recess teacher in charge, who after hearing my story, summarily marched me into Mr. Cheney's office. Engulfed in super-charged terror, I was barely able to deliver my tale.

In response, and quite surprising, Principal Cheney cracked a smile and reached for his phone. "Mrs. Leader, this is Mr. Cheney. I want to tell you that Gerry just swallowed a train wheel," and with that he let out a contagious belly laugh that wouldn't stop and enveloped me. Soon I was laughing, too. The crisis was over. (For the record, let it be known that everything came out all right.)

My gratitude club has to include Father Flanagan, although we never met. Our connection came via Mary Huskin, a dirty blond with a bleached front lock. She was a real looker that I spotted the first day of my high school freshman year. Her Christian cross necklace gave her away as a St. Mary's junior high school graduate, the parochial school down the block.

As she fumbled with the handle on her hallway locker, I asked, "Can I help?"

When she turned to answer, I hopelessly fell under her spell. My gaze then, and subsequently, couldn't detach from her luscious red lips that she periodically moistened with a licking tongue. Transfixed, it took only two weeks before Mary was cuddled next to me in my dad's dusty-green DeSoto on a Friday night. (Anticipating the big night out, each of the chrome fins protruding from the rear fenders, had been repeatedly polished to a gleaming reflection.)

The setting was the parking lot at the Forest Park Lily Pond overlook that demanded early arrival to find a smooching spot.

In hardly any time at all, the two of us were kissing. This was a first-time experience for both of us, and it was rapturous, but next morning's phone call revealed mutual feelings of guilt.

What to do? Keep in mind, this was the '50s; I was not to be easily denied those ever-so-inviting lips. Mary's idea was heaven-struck. We would have fun on Friday night, she would go to confession on Saturday, the priest would absolve us of our sins of lust, and Sunday we would be made holy again by taking communion. Our plan was that every week it would be the same routine, but Mary's idea lasted just one week.

It was nixed by the priest who said that my sins couldn't be purged because I wasn't a Catholic and Mary's confession would be suspect if not inauthentic. Father Flanagan, it turned out, was the priest hearing Mary's confession on Saturday. Recognizing her voice at Sunday's Mass, he took her aside and advised her that everything above the neck was okay, but below was dangerous territory. Mary and I took this as good news and remained devoted to kisses the remainder of our relationship.

But Coach Wallack has the last words. Late spring of my sophomore year, I burst my denial bubble and had to confront the fact that I was a "nobody" at Maplewood Richmond Heights Senior High School. Everybody but me was being invited to big parties where cheerleaders and jocks wore letter sweaters and were the center of attention. The queens and kings of the junior and senior proms were the big athletes. Next year I wasn't going to be left out. I had to have a letter sweater and that meant going out for varsity football in the fall. Mom and all my non-athletic friends thought I was crazy because I hadn't participated in freshman or Junior Varsity Football.

Coach Wallack with his pointy head, toothy smiles, and fat arms, said, "The other players will maul you and eat you up!"

My famous soft hands, even bathed in silver nitrate to harden them, were raw hamburger after each practice. Sure enough, grandmaster Wallack flashed his evil smile and never let up. I paid dearly for not coming out for football two years earlier.

"Leader, you lazy-foot, move; move your sweet ass and hit."

Of course, the opening game of the season he appointed me to the goon squad that races down the field after the kick off, sacrificing themselves as targets for the opponents' defense men to mow down as they protect the ball carrier. Supercharged with beginner's adrenaline, I flashed down the field only to find myself paralyzed, deer-caught-in-the-headlights, not 5 feet from the ball carrier who equally startled, ceased his motion and stared at me.

Our locked-in-place drama ended when Coach Wallack yelled loud enough for the public address system to amplify his voice even further, "Leader, God dammit, this is football; tackle the son of a bitch!"

No other instructions were needed. I did - to much cheering and fan appreciation. Coach Wallack even slapped me on the butt when I came back to the sidelines. I earned and wore my varsity letter, and it proudly sits (75 years later), in my cabinet of wonders — prized memorabilia. Happily ever after, and during my junior and senior years, I was named a prince at both junior and senior proms.

THE 'INDIAN' ROOM

THE MOST UNIQUE ROOM I ever stayed in as a kid was filled with scary images, pictures of a place I'd never been, but it was also really cozy and comfortable. The deep-pillowed couch would envelope me when I burrowed into it. I'm remembering the stomach-tensing feeling upon entering my paternal grandparents' 'Indian' Room in their home in Centralia, Missouri. Probably no more than 150 square feet in size, they had filled it from floor to ceiling with Indigenous American artifacts from their 30 years in Idaho in the early 1900s. Every other weekend during my childhood, my family and I made the 256.4-mile round trip from Richmond Heights, where I lived, to Centralia. On Fridays, I couldn't wait to go.

I'd want to go in the room and, at the same time, I was afraid to. Never would I venture going inside it at night; the bloodstains on the stone hatchet alone were enough to keep me away. Then there were photos of warriors with bows and arrows seeming to point directly at me. Looking down, Geronimo, with his weathered face and piercing eyes, never stopped staring into my eyes. I imagined riding one of his horses but I couldn't ride bareback. Maybe he would capture me and one of his braves could teach me.

Oh, that was a scary daydream, but exciting! I always traveled to another world when I visited their 'Indian' Room.

AN ADOLESCENT AWAKENING

FROM SEVENTH TO TENTH GRADE, I spent two months of my summers at Camp Miniwanca on the shores of Lake Michigan in northern Michigan. I was successively a camper, camp leader, camp counselor, and finally, on the camp work staff (first, preparing five gallons of soup daily for junior campers, then as waterfront director). Camp Miniwanca was founded by William H. Danforth, a son of a Louisiana sharecropper, who became the entrepreneur who created the Ralston Purina Company, makers of pet chows, farm feeds, and Wheat Chex. The camp's ideology, based on Danforth's life story, was to live a four-square life: social, physical, mental, and religious.

During my second year in the Senior Boys unit, I was chosen Tribe Leader. This was unexpected and, at the time, I thought, undeserved. I had never distinguished myself in any activity, yet here I was leading others.

It was not my only awakening. For three summers, my constant companion, and as it turned out, my 'older woman' guide-to-life was Liz, four years my senior and in college while I was still in high school. A remarkable relationship, it changed the trajectory of my life. There was the budding adolescent sexual component, but it went no further than heavy kissing. The relationship had much more complexity and mystery. As one whose literary repertoire had never gone beyond Mickey Spillane quarter novels, I was transfixed when she read Steinbeck short stories to me in a canoe in the middle of the camp's lake. We enjoyed long swims, sails, and walks, and sometimes sat quietly, the two of us alone, at sunset in Miniwanca's enormous and spectacularly beautiful outdoor chapel. We soulfully listened to each other and played together.

It was transforming. No one had ever confirmed and blessed me as she did, and as did the whole camp experience. I returned summer after summer until I made the mistake of mixing my camp world and my home world by inviting Liz to my house for a Christmas holiday.

Unfortunately, a change in season, locale…the relationship dissolved. But not the effect on me; that has been everlasting.

THE ORACLE

J.K. HOUSEMAN LOOMED LARGE IN my life on August 6, 1956. I was between junior and senior years in an engineering curriculum at Iowa State College of Agriculture and Engineering in Ames, Iowa. Mr. Houseman, an Iowa State graduate of some 20 years earlier and then a senior vice president at General Electric's Large Turbine Division, had located a summer job in GE's Chicago headquarters for me.

My internship over, he invited me to lunch at his exclusive men's club, The Oracle, at the top of a building in the heart of Chicago's Financial District. I was very pleased with the invitation; it was the opportunity I had been waiting for. I was going to request a full-time job at GE in June, 1957, after my graduation. I twitched with both excitement and concern. I kept picturing a cartoonish newspaper headline that characterized my aspiration and self-doubt: "Cow College graduate attempts move to larger and greener pastures, but does he have the right stuff?"

Meeting day. Once inside the elevator, the attendant spied me as a newbie to the building. I was fitfully fingering through a ragged spiral notebook.

"Can I help you?" he asked.

"Yes," I replied. "Where is the Oracle Club?"

"It's on the 25th floor and I will get you there safe and sound."

Well, that was a relief. I had never met J.K. Houseman. All of our correspondence had been by U.S. mail. He was waiting at "his" table. At least six and a half feet tall with a firm grip,

Mr. Houseman was outfitted in a double breasted, well-tailored silk suit with a color-coordinated rep tie and highly polished black loafers. My shlumpy cotton sports jacket and beige khaki trousers were a notable contrast.

I was graciously received by Mr. Houseman but flummoxed by his offer of a martini with a special dry gin found only at The Oracle Club. My alcohol history had been limited to 3.2% beer, but here it was, the test. Was I ready to move up with the big city boys? The martini tasted damn good and went down quickly. Two swallows, gone! J.K, as I was instructed to call him, fed me compliments on my performance during the summer that he had picked up from my supervisors. I tingled with pride; I was on a high. Halfway through lunch, J.K. volunteered that he was having a second drink and would I as well? It would have been impolite to decline his offer. This time I tasted and enjoyed the sacred gin, and I told J.K so.

The luncheon was over before I knew it. I didn't want it to end. I was in happy land. J.K thought a full-time job at GE was a real possibility. He excused himself to visit the restroom and suggested we meet at the elevators. Sitting there for a few minutes, I started to feel faint and a little dizzy. I thought, "The elevator seems a long way away; I better get started."

Struggling to get up from my chair, I momentarily collapsed, then tried again. Half way up, I reached out and grabbed the back of the high-back chair at the neighboring table. They looked startled, but smiled. I looked for the next chair to claim on the path to the elevator. I threaded from chair to chair, first thinking, "Who will take me?" I reached for the next chair. "Where can I go?" Next chair. "Boeing?" Next chair. "Honeywell?"

Arriving at the elevators, I encountered the attendant I had met earlier. He was standing by an open elevator door, and ushered me in. J.K. was not in sight. Good thing, as I was in no condition to say my "thank you's" and "goodbyes." The elevator ride down was periodically interrupted by stops at floors where there were no passengers either exiting or entering. Upon arrival at the ground floor, the attendant spontaneously directed me to a "staff only" rest facility.

I wrote a letter to J.K apologizing for not having the opportunity to thank him for the enjoyable and stimulating luncheon at The Oracle. His return correspondence thanked me for being willing to discuss my summer experience at GE. He assured me there would be a position available after graduation.

Such was not my fate. In June, 1957, I was commissioned as Second Lieutenant in the U.S. Army Corps of Engineers and called up for active duty that November, precluding work at GE.

Post Script

One unanswerable question has remained with me for years: "Was it J.K. who, trying to spare me embarrassment, arranged for the elevator attendant to assist me on the journey to ground level and then provide me with the staff bathroom safe haven? Or had it been the attendant's spontaneous act of kindness?"

THEY, THEM, AND ME

WE DIDN'T SHARE A GREAT relationship at the beginning. Probably due to a total lack of contact. The first thing I remember hearing about them: they went to a trashy school in a trashy part of town.

I'd never even spoken with any of *them* until my junior year in college. It was the 1950s, in middle America. *They* were going to be evicted from *their* urban renewal apartments. I was hired to measure the size and assess the value of the spaces in order to compensate *their* landlords.

Surprisingly, *they* put me at ease. After an anxiety-provoking knock at each of *their* doors, they were friendly, helpful, and even funny; they offered me food. I mostly turned *them* down on mom's advice: "You never know if the food has been refrigerated or whether or not *they* have washed *their* dishes!" But I sneaked barbecue every Friday afternoon with the Thomas clan and had great times.

Iowa State College of Agriculture and Engineering, 6,000 students strong, in 1953, had not one of *them* in sight. Fort Leonard Wood, Missouri, was *their* territory, that is, all of the soldiers' and sergeants', but officers like me were all White. Lined up on the parade grounds for my introduction as company commanding officer, I looked out and thought, "My God, the majority are *them*!"

Master Sergeant Marcel (White), the head non-commissioned officer in the company, heard of my not-too-subtle prejudice, and arranged for successive Black sergeants to lead my platoons of soldiers in measured training exercises. I finally succumbed to the belief that skin color didn't predict competence.

Racial walls in my mind began to crumble, and major bricks plummeted down when things got personal. Norwinna May occupied an office roughly equal to her boss, a vice president of Gulf Oil Company in Pittsburgh, with a presence that exceeded his. Curvaceous and glamorously garbed, she appeared to me like a Black beauty prize for a bachelor consultant, ready to prove his manhood after a recent divorce.

After a month-long whirlwind tour of Black-dominated jazz clubs, dance halls, and out of the way soulful joints, she split the atom with an inquiry. "Is it my novelty, or is it me?"

It took another month for an answer, it took another month for me to connect with Norwinna May. And it took another month for us to decide it wasn't for the long term.

Interestingly, it was a Black man, A. B. Corcoran, who was the unexpected heavy competition for the hand of my wife, Lucy. One Sunday afternoon, when Lucy was in her stopwatch period of suitors, I met A. B. leaving her apartment as I was coming in. Lucy introduced this tall, thin, bearded, handsome Black man whose demeanor made you feel honored to be in his proximity. Not by his intention, but because of who he was. After Lucy and I became a committed couple, we continued our friendship and personal connection with A. B. which continued to help me see beyond his skin color.

When I look back over my life and explore my feelings and opinions about race (something that isn't often encouraged in today's world), questions arise: Why did Black apartment dwellers have to offer tasty barbecue to win my approval? Why did Black sergeants have to demonstrate their competence to qualify as humans in my head? Why did Norwinna May question my motives? Why did A. B. Corcoran have to be a competitor for Lucy to win my attention and eventual friendship?

Conclusion: I've carried and am carrying a load of prejudice that warrants continuing reflection.

BREAKING OUT

DELTA QUEEN
OH YE OF LITTLE FAITH

IT'S 1972, I'M IN NEW Orleans, the only city where Tennessee Williams said you could be truly yourself. I'm a three-month refugee from a prior marriage, longing for my two daughters, Jody and Kristin, who are living in Lexington, Massachusetts and recently driven from my prior academic position by a dean who thought the first Earth Day in 1971 (which I had organized), was a pile of crap waiting for disposal.

I'm in my second-floor office at Tulane Business School conscientiously grading papers and preparing for next morning's 8 am class. Storm Edith had missed New Orleans, but its side effects showered the city with heavy winds and rain. The sun was peeking through bilious clouds as I look out my window. The last of my colleagues left the building hours ago. New Orlean nights, I've learned, use storms as an excuse to sip sugary Sazerac, and slurp oysters on the half shell, dappled with fiery hot sauce. Jim in the next office, on his way out, had ominously warned of a possible second storm that comes from temporarily being in the eye followed by being whiplashed by the back of the storm's circle of winds.

I hunker down. The phone rings. Barbara, my newfound girlfriend, an incurable romantic, knows me well enough that she would find me in my office.

"Let's take a drive up the river and visit Oak Alley. I've never been there and I know you haven't. I promise at least half a dozen rainbows," she says.

"Can't. I've got an 8:00 and papers to return."

She replies, "Can I take you seriously, or are you a one-month stand?"

Thirty minutes later, I'm at her almost morosely dark apartment with a slowly lapping ceiling fan distributing smells of dank drapes and a tattered Persian rug on the floor, exuding the super sweet aroma of dried magnolia petals littering the floor beneath at least fifteen slowly dying plants.

We are an improbable pairing: an overly responsible midwesterner tempered by East Coast cynicism trying to work himself out of emotional bankruptcy, paired with a willowy Lauren Bacall blonde with a face announcing past pain endured. Similar to the city of which she is a product, she personifies fragility and vulnerability which more than thirty years later, Katrina will confirm. Barbara has learned that despite hardships, life should be lived to its fullest and enjoyed. I think of her as my teacher.

We go no more than ten miles up the winding river road that tracks the levied Mississippi twenty feet above us when I have to stop. Barbara really doesn't know how far away Oak Alley is, plus I am hungry and my tank is one-quarter full. The Shell station looks like it hasn't seen a customer in a month. I have observed that the decay process in New Orleans is accelerated by the lack of motion of everybody and everything. I pump only a half tank of gas, worried that the underground containers may be corroded, allowing water into the gas, but I'm desperate.

I go back to the car with two soggy, home-made oatmeal cookies I had spied in the back room, mercifully given to me by the proprietor when he couldn't deliver on my request for peanut butter Cheez-Its. (That was sometime well before I knew they were junk food.)

Barbara swears we are headed in the right direction, but the deckhand on the car ferry doesn't recognize the name Oak Alley. He does, however, believe there is some old plantation up the road. Barbara, without any apparent better information, assuredly corrects him, saying it is only two or three miles more. The dark cloud over Baton Rouge, thirty miles to the north, adds to my anxiety that I will be empty-handed and empty-minded tomorrow morning when and if I get to class. But there is no turning back.

One hour and sixteen miles from the ferry, under ominous storm clouds, we pull into an alley of fifty or more moss-laden oaks, arching across a drive to a three-storied, neo-colonial plantation which puts Tara's from *Gone with the Wind* to shame. Arriving at the adjacent parking lot, we are confronted with a sign:

> Closed. No Trespassing

I think, well isn't this the completion of a God-damned day.

The one car in the parking lot has black and white markings like a patrol car. I immediately begin my rehearsal of an explanation for our innocent trespassing. My heart is pounding and I'm fearful we will finish the evening in a country jail.

Upon our approach however, the car lurches forward and becomes recognizable as a New Orleans taxi, some sixty miles from its home. In the passenger seat, not the back seat, sits a woman who Barbara announces looks very pained.

"How can you tell?" I ask.

"I don't know. She just looks desperate. We have to follow them."

We trail them back down the oak-arched roadway across the highway and into an open field of overgrown grass, bouncing and bumping our way as in a B-movie, cops and robbers' pursuit. The taxi screeches to a halt not five feet away from a four-foot-high ornate iron fence which probably, a hundred years ago, separated the plantation from the cotton fields.

Barbara and I watch, paralyzed by indecision as the Black driver pushes the elderly woman and her black valise over the fence and then follows her as they run toward the river.

"Enough, enough," I argue. "Let's get out of here. The lady climbed the fence of her own volition."

"How do you know? Aren't you curious? Are you scared?"

We follow them. One-hundred yards toward the river, panting and exhausted from our quickened pace, we come upon a most unexpected and curious scene. The woman is perched on her valise, relaxed as a train-station regular, gazing toward the river.

She slowly turns to us. "Join us; we are waiting for the Delta Queen."

Her co-conspirator chimes in, "The storm, it made for a late start, but she'll be coming soon."

To say I am stupefied is an understatement. How am I to believe that these two solitary figures, in an open field in the middle of the night, are waiting for a boat with no levy or dock in sight? It risks my sanity. Am I in a Pinter play and don't know it?

They have a story for their mutual madness. She is the medical physician on the paddle-wheeler, but her plane was delayed landing in New Orleans, because of the storm, Edith, and she had even missed the Delta Queen's delayed departure.

OK. That has a degree of credibility, but the supposed taxi driver phoning the steamboat pilot before the boat left New

Orleans, suggesting they meet them at this forlorn, jungled and brambled location is beyond belief.

Barbara now presents as another co-conspirator. She will hear nothing of my entreaties to leave. "You can go. But I'm staying," she states.

My guilt in leaving my date in a desolate field with at least one delusional man trumps my better judgment. It doesn't preclude me from investigating whether or not there is a landing or dock to transfer the good doctor on to the boat if it should show up.

Thirty minutes later, slightly bloodied and with water-soaked shoes, I pronounce to the assembled three, that there are rotten vestiges of what appears to be a dock, but it is well over thirty feet inland from any water and completely encased with shrubs and swamp maples. No way any boat of any size is going to approach it. The three are unmoved and with dwindling polite conversation, the four of us take silent sentry on the horizon waiting for an imaginary vessel. I, too, have become enveloped in this collective conspiracy. Why else would I give myself over to this absurd situation?

Fireflies are a temporary relief from the monotony. They are briefly seen as distant markers of an oncoming boat. When a narrow beam does present itself down river, I at first dismiss it as an aberration, until several more illuminate the path of a dual-stacked wedding cake paddle-wheeler closing in on us, draped in colored lights. Even then, I am in disbelief. It must be a mirage, a figment of my now-seduced imagination. But it is real and headed in our direction.

"How will they know where we are? We don't even have a flashlight," I exclaim.

The taxi driver assures us, "The pilot will know."

Sure enough, a search beam finds me frantically waving while the others appear undisturbed by the fast closing of the steamer.

Aboard, partying is in progress with muffled sounds of Dixieland wafting through the air. Passengers lean over guard rails, drinks in hand, gaping at the change of course the boat has taken, which now stops twenty feet short of the shore.

The doctor brushes herself off, smooths back her hair, and the taxicab driver trails her, valise in hand. They both walk toward the river.

Alright, they would use a life boat to fetch the doctor, right? No. A gang plank reaching from the deck to the pilot's roost begins to slowly make its way down to the landing with search lights following its path. Its destination is ten feet from the doctor, standing with her valise. She steps forward, mounting the gang plank and with queenly steps, slowly and triumphantly traverses to the Delta Queen amid the cheers and toasts of her admiring subjects.

I stand transfixed, still in disbelief. If I'm not in a play, perhaps a movie. The gang plank is raised, but the ceremony is not over, nor is the disillusion of my cynicism that magic is possible if only you believe hard enough. The Delta Queen backs out of her imaginary harbor and turns downstream with a calliope in its stern, puffing out different colored steam for every note and makes its way up river.

> *Boo ba-doop-a-doop, boop boo doo.*
> *Boo ba-doop-a-doop, boop boo doo.*

Preparing for Saihoji Temple

Anumber of years ago, in the middle of August, I found myself sitting, cross legged and barefoot on a polished hardwood floor in a Buddhist temple in Kyoto, Japan, with twenty or so other tourists, most of whom were Japanese. It must have been at least 120 degrees, and with the humidity, I saturated every piece of my clothing with perspiration. I labored to be quiet and motionless. I sat there for at least forty-five minutes, each minute more excruciating than the previous one. The silence was periodically broken by a chanting Zen Buddhist priest. My mind raced, a cacophony of thoughts, the essence of which was: how could I leave without being disrespectful or annoying others?

I had come to see the gardens at Saihoji (translated into English as Moss Temple), a UNESCO World Heritage Site. Comprised of more than 120 varieties of moss, Saihoji was founded 1300 years ago and refurbished, alongside its temple, in 1969.

Unlike the other Kyoto gardens I had visited, admission to Saihoji appeared organized to frustrate only the most determined visitor. I was required to apply for admission, by mail, months in advance. The entrance was unmarked, difficult to find, and abutted a noisy, crowded highway, belching noxious automobile fumes. Upon entering, I was startled by an enveloping silence and peace and ushered into the temple which stood between the gate and the moss garden.

It was there, where I was about to expire, well past the time I thought I could stand up and walk, where my mind and body finally gave up. My muscles relaxed and my psychic chatter dissipated. Sweaty, unfulfilled, and disappointed, I could feel my body reluctantly yield to the hardwood floor. I became present. Perhaps it was coincidence, but I believe it was planned: my yielding to being in the moment coincided with a Buddhist priest beckoning us into the moss garden.

This was my fourth Kyoto garden in a week, but this time I didn't just witness its beauty, which had been my exclusive reward from the other three. I experienced Saihoji differently. Rather than the garden being an object to be inspected, I was captured by it. I became *part* of the garden.

Saihoji has lived in me since. Its earthy fragrances, contemplative silence, tactile moistness, and visual images, now over 20 years old, are as sensorially vivid as the day I walked its paths and sat on its boulders. I believe the secret was in the preparation. My somewhat tortured encapsulation in the temple had a purpose: to ready me for Saihoji, to bring me into 'presence.' I could then, and only then, follow the reverential footsteps of the priests who have nurtured the moss for almost 1300 years. I was being prepared to become a steward of earth's delicate and fragile beauty, forever entrusted to my care.

HONOR

I WAS IN A TRAVELING PARTY of five, including four women, hosted by my wife Lucy, visiting old friends, temples, and sacred music festivals for the month of February in Southern India.

Lucy had learned from previous travels and curating art in Southern India, a particular location that might prove personally meaningful and a beautiful site to visit. We'd see a collection of handcrafted terracotta horses that indigenous people, starting centuries before, had created to spiritually protect their villages. Twenty-three years ago, on my first trip to India with Lucy and our teacher-guide, Sunithi Narayan, I remembered seeing a half a dozen or so such sites in forests outside rural villages, but this particular site promised something more. Just what was unclear.

The location was isolated; our minivan driver needed directions from several locals before we pulled up to a path leading into a forest, announced by a large, highly-decorated, stand-alone portal that could easily accommodate a moving van. Two richly painted, two-foot square pillars, at least 15 feet high, were entrusted with supporting a horizontal crossbeam displaying an extraordinary collection of painted ceramic figures, deities and elephants. It was an oddity presenting itself unexpectedly out of nowhere. If it was an entrance, entrance to what? The 'what' must be big if the size and elaborateness of the portal was any indication.

Shandi, from Delhi (who had joined our group the day before on the suggestion of a mutual friend), and I were first off the van. We went through the portal and found ourselves in the middle of an allée of terracotta, half-size horses nestled next to each other, cheek by jowl: plump, some smiling, some with menacing teeth, some who earlier had been enlivened with now fading paint. The majority were crumbling with the weight of history. The horses were expected, but not hundreds, perhaps thousands, as far as an eye's view could reach.

Shandi and I sauntered, gazing side-to-side, around a bend in the path where we were surprised to be confronted by a life-sized, terracotta elephant, painted blue, with golden clay bells surrounding her neck.

After the elephant, another shock. Two men came from around the other side of the elephant. A bare-chested, elderly man wrapped from the waist down in a white dhoti kept his distance; but the other, a villager in western dress wearing a striped t-shirt and khaki pants accosted us with a snarling face. Angrily issuing guttural sounds, he challenged us with non-verbal gestures to remove our shoes.

Shandi shouted, "No way, no way am I going to give up my shoes!" and she walked away.

My teeth clenched, left alone, too stunned to move, I stood paralyzed, my mind flashing PowerPoint explanations: Locals terrorize tourists; without shoes you can't escape; must stand my ground, my wallet is next.

I found my hand patting my left rear pocket where I keep my wallet. But with a momentary reflection, I rejected this possibility of a personal heist. Why was I resisting? He kept pointing to my shoes. It felt like the two of us were in a competition, a standoff, ego versus ego.

Precipitously, Lucy arrived on the scene and suggested that there was probably something worth seeing at the end of the path. Following her example, I took off my shoes, and my antagonist quickly departed. Lucy left me to explore on my own while she attended to the others in my party, and I proceeded down the path.

An unexplained positive feeling invaded my being. Looking down, I noticed the path had recently been broom swept of leaves and debris. My subconscious had beat out my consciousness in calculating that it was unlikely hustlers after my shoes or money would be engaged in such beautifying.

Here, many of the terracotta horses lining the path were more richly decorated, indicating more recent servicing. I entered a large clearing, hosted by another enormous terracotta elephant, at least twice the size of the one visited earlier. This one held a platform jammed with cartoon-like ceramic characters, each vying for my attention. Their exclamatory paint job announced that this was an important place.

The ground at the far end of the clearing was populated by a dozen or so stone-carved squat deities, each wrapped in white shrouds that had clearly been touched by others. On the foreheads of their elf-like heads were displayed red and white flowers. Behind this front line, hundreds more, smaller-sized deities appeared ready to sacrifice themselves in the battle for my gaze. Why was I the center of attention? As a shudder raced down my spine, I felt vulnerable.

So absorbed in making meaning of the terracotta figures, I was only vaguely aware that others had joined me in the clearing. I recognized Lucy's and my lady travel companions' voices in the conversational buzz but paid little attention until Lucy unexpectedly came up from behind me and whispered in my ear, "Look up, look up!"

It hit me. "Oh my God, it is THE tree, a sacred Tamarind worshiped by Indigenous people!" Preposterously large, it stood seven or eight stories high, dominating the clearing in which I was standing. I felt dwarfed when I fully absorbed its presence. The juxtaposition of my being unaware of its presence and then the jolt of realization transfixed me.

I will never know if what happened next was or was not by pure chance or a spiritually-guided intervention. The bare-chested elder in his white dhoti walked directly in front of me, not an arm's length away. At first, I was startled, but at his invitational nod, to which I agreed, he pressed on my forehead, just above my nose, a finger-sized spot of white sandalwood paste. I felt blessed!

I was not alone. Others in our party, as well as a busload of devotees, populated the clearing, receiving this priest's spiritual anointing. The Sacred Tree Temple was at work.

But the final blessings of the morning visit to the Sacred Tree Temple were administered by Barbara, one of my travel companions, on her walk back to the van. She came across the western-dressed villager, who had persisted in my shoe removal. Attempting to talk with him, she realized he was deaf. She spoke to him in international sign language. He appreciatively reciprocated, smiled, and acknowledged the gift she had presented to him.

Unfortunately, I did not have the opportunity to make my peace with him and express my own gratitude for his guardianship of the Sacred Tree Temple. But I think he knew we all had a uniquely meaningful spiritual experience.

ELDERS

IT IS JULY, 1994. I am standing with Lucy, 10-year-old Wren, and a family of close friends at the edge of a circle of over 50 red-robed, chanting Maasai tribesmen and women. We are on a camping trip in Tanzania, East Africa, on the Serengeti plain, to view star-quality wild animals and explosively colored birds.

One of our trip guides is a Maasai who has led us into this apparent ceremony, but without explanation as to its purpose. I do feel an aura of welcomeness preempting my initial anxiety. I feel included. I am moved by a spiritual reflection, when the seniors tell the Maasai origin story that is accomplished through three language translations.

My surprising involvement in the service is unnerving and unexpected. The subject is cows, the sacred mammals of nourishment and economic value in the Maasai community. One's status in the community is calibrated on how many cows you own.

"Does any one of our guests have cows?" we are asked.

The only response to the question is silence, but I think: Wouldn't the cattle on my grandpapi's farm in Missouri qualify?

I raise my hand and the assembled take a deep collective breath. "How many?"

"Twenty or so," I answer, which is followed by restless conversation among the assembled.

Senior Maasai confer with one another, and a stool is placed in the center of the circle. I'm invited to come forth and take a place of honor. I'm bewildered, nervous, and come close to sliding off the stool while I attempt to answer questions and describe my herd. After each of my responses, there are collective positive sighs. That is, until I confess that the herd is in the States, and not with me in the immediate vicinity.

The nonverbal, muted hissing signals their disappointment, but I am still the center of attention. I sense, during the subsequent questioning, that my exalted status is about to be eclipsed.

"Who is caring for the herd?"

"My brother," I answer.

"Who is the oldest?"

When I answer, "I am," I know I am taking my leave.

They continue with the ceremony, but ignore me, sitting alone, disgraced, in the middle of the circle.

First born males never leave their family's cows to the care of their brothers, that's a sacrilege.

ORIGINS OF EVERYDAY BEAUTY

LUCY AND I HAVE COME to Orissa, India's least developed state, to visit prehistoric tribes, who have been only marginally touched by India's modern society and economy. We are interested in their Indigenous crafts and have a long-time interest and collection of 'unschooled,' sometimes called 'outsider,' art. On previous trips to India, we have collected tribal drawings, weavings, and lost-wax brass castings that have made their way through middlemen to the retail marketplace in India. Four years ago, Lucy was thwarted in her attempt to visit tribal areas; this year she will have her chance. India seems to be the ideal place to see, and perhaps purchase, spontaneous artistic creations of people sheltered from outside influences. We are on the hunt for the origins of everyday beauty.

Our guide in Orissa is Krish Krishnan, a native of Chennai and a former commander in the Indian Navy. He's the son of our first teacher-guide in India in 1998, Sunithi Narayan. Krish had scouted the tribal areas of Orissa once before and located a knowledgeable and skilled guide, Bubbly, who spoke a bit of English, and was articulate in Hindi, but knew many native dialects of the tribals. Having grown up in an Indian village situated close by several tribal villages, he frequently escorted "outsiders" to them, being trusted and quite familiar with their customs.

Lucy, Krish, Bubbly, and I visit six tribal villages. They vary according to the degree in which the national and Orissian governments have intervened in their lives, attempting to "mainstream" them into contemporary Indian society. All have been touched in some way, but there are wide differences in their receptivity to outsiders and how much their lives have been affected by the contact. All of the tribes, no matter how remote, expect payment of about 10 rupee, or 25 cents, for having their pictures taken. The rupee payment is in exchange for their time posing for a picture.

Our experience commences with visiting two of the six tribes. They represent the extremes of what I observe.

We approach a thatched-roof, adobe-walled village built on a mountain slope. It looks like everyone lives in one of two very long houses extending up the hill, but you can see that there are separate entrances and thus, partitioned living spaces under the overhang. It's 10 am and save for a lone man silently passing us, with no recognition on his part, we appear to be the only ones present. He will be the only man we see on our visit to this village.

We have traveled 20 miles on dirt and partially-tarred roads from the nearest small town to this remote sight, only to be confronted with a government-engineered, foot-thick, twelve-feet wide, seventy-yards-long road leading up the slope of the mountain to the village. Bubbly says it is expected to keep the village from sliding into the creek below during monsoon season. The incongruity of concrete walls shoved cheek-by-jowl to a tribal village is distracting.

Bubbly has instructed us to only take pictures of men and women when he has received permission. Led by him, we trail through the lanes and small passages looking for someone, anyone. No one is to be found. This village is apparently empty. It feels like a hollow and desolate village-scape, where our own footsteps make the only recognizable sounds on the baked-clay ground. Finally, a small boy of six in a traditional loin cloth, starts trailing us. A crudely-shaped, metal ring is persistently offered to us for sale. Bubbly dismisses the proposed transaction.

In the meantime, we stumble upon two older, squatting women draped in hand-spun white cloth, whose threads have been woven from the bark of an indigenous tree. Bubbly greets them on our behalf, but there is little direct acknowledgement of us on their part. Their eyes tell us we are intruders, but we might bring rupee. Several other women emerge from dark passages, squat, and inspect our white skin, Lucy's red hair, and the photographic equipment from another civilization. Their skin is ebony, their only ornamentation, a metal, two-inch ring piercing each of their noses. It would seem we haven't interrupted any routine; they are quite content to bargain over small, metal cooking instruments, a rough-hewn knife, and a very plain bracelet. The negotiations end in a stalemate. The asking price in rupees is too steep in Bubbly's estimation.

After several hasty photos, Bubbly finishes our encounter by distributing the obligatory 10-rupee notes. We hurry down the hill, I, with a bitter aftertaste, feeling like I used to as a child when I had done something naughty and wanted to run away from it.

Reaching the concrete pavement felt reassuring – I was once again in familiar 'civilized' territory. I feel even better rubbing my hands with Purell, an antibacterial crème before eating my biscuits from a sanitary-foiled package.

Escaping in our car, we watch village women silently assemble to receive the government's weekly allotment of rice. Bubbly thinks the men are probably off brewing a fermented tree root, combined with pineapple juice, to concoct a powerful alcoholic beverage to drink, then feed to their families - young and old alike – and to use for barter with other tribes. We all feel like intruders, and there is silence as we drive away until Bubbly starts an animated conversation about our next tribal visit.

The following day, as we drive to a second village, Bubbly is quite upbeat. He is going home. The small Indian community where he was raised is only five miles away from this tribe and he, as a youth, had made frequent visits there. This Indigenous community had made the transition from hunting-and-gathering to agriculture several generations earlier, but has fiercely kept their independence and cultural integrity, rejecting government assistance. They've kept their distance from the nearby village and any government incursions into their life.

The thatched-roof, square huts are grouped around family courtyards with woven-reed fences draped with brightly colored swaths of material set out to dry. Most family units contain three or four wives and children under the husbandry of one man. Each wife and her offspring have their own hut.

The baked-clay courtyards are immaculate and highlighted by the multicolored drapes that surround them. They are dotted with circular straw-woven trays of millet, rice, and assorted seeds baking in the sun. The placement of the reflective disks of grains could have been bathers in a Caribbean resort, artfully distributed around the central courtyard. After viewing several of such spaces, there is no question that these are not random placements, but intentional compositions.

Approaching one compound of Bubbly's choosing, I hear the muffled sounds of a rhythmic pounding, inviting a closer inspection. One wife seated, her legs surrounding a wooden bowl approximately two feet in circumference, repeatedly and rhythmically rams a double-sized-like baseball bat to crumble kernels. Her exposed biceps rival the sinuous muscles of a training gym denizen, man or woman. Dressed in a lime green sari, highlighted by a regal purple scarf, she smiles in our direction, recognizing Bubbly, but not interrupting her syncopated beat.

Bubbly tells us that they, like the previous tribe, have a long history of wearing white cloth made from organic material, but have colored their costumes with naturally-made dyes. Another wife, clearly the older of the three, is being assisted in another hut by a daughter, who stands behind her mother and grasps the handle just above her mother's hand, their multicolored saris waving at us like the soft lapping of butterfly wings with each stroke. Bubbly translates a conversation with a third wife, sifting the grain from the chafe with a woven screen as she speaks. This is a twice-a-day ritual, 365 days in the year, between gathering, cooking, feeding, mending, and tending to the children.

There is a quiet and Spartan order to the village and village life. The women have their roles and the men tend to the fields. They worship nature and their common open-air amphitheater has as its focus, a wizened tree decorated with vines and sacred stones.

Everyday beauty is a product of women. Male artists are not in evidence in our brief visit, although the wooden door of the chief's hut is highly decorated and affixed with at least four brass hasps. Who is responsible for the decoration is not clear. The bold, geometric painted designs in ochre, white, black, and burnt umber on the adobe walls of the village are a product of the women's efforts.

During our walking tour, we come upon a woman perched halfway up a triangular-shaped wooden step ladder, washing her wall with a rag that's been dipped in a wooden bowl of liquid burnt umber. Weekly, she reports, she repaints the triangular and square design on her home. She is clearly proud of her work and her work exhibits her pride.

Bubbly wants us to appreciate how important ornamentation is in the life of the tribe's women. He has a particularly close friendship with two older women, both of whom look, by our calibration of wrinkles, about eighty years old, but Bubbly informs us they are in their late fifties. We experience first-hand the ten-pound weight of each of the two tubular, metal necklaces each of them wears. At Bubbly's bidding, one raises her pink sari to expose a reed back-brace, worn to offset the twenty-pound weight carried around her neck. The shiny, metal necklaces symbolize the woman's status, but also represent the value the community places on beauty. There is no need to purchase tribal artifacts here, nor are they on sale. The beauty of their village is value enough.

A day later, after our visit, prompted by an innocent question on my part, Bubbly finally admits that our peaceable entry and exit into the village was more problematic than we had assumed. Apparently, this tribe is not reluctant to aggressively ward off unwelcomed visitors. Last year, government officials in a misguided attempt to make a photo ID for each of them, had set about taking individual pictures, but refused to pay the traditional 10-rupee fee to each – a practice they had learned from other tribes and come to expect. After smashing the government's cameras, they took up their bows and arrows and chased the officials away. None of the government photographers were killed, but several were injured from arrow wounds. Bubbly's postscript is unsettling, even as an afterthought, but in retrospect, probably essential to our appreciation of them as creative people protecting their culture.

Lady in Red – Finding My Van Gogh

WE ARE SHADOWED BY A line of sycamores at the edge of an olive grove. Their silvery leaves shimmer with an uneven syncopation. The rosé is dry and earthy. With a bite, the baguettes crunch and expose their treats: fresh tomatoes and basil and local cheese. We are a seven-years-young storytelling group lying in triangulated space, steeping our private thoughts as we listen to our spiritual leader, Jay O'Callahan.

On his knees, he is reading aloud Van Gogh's 1889 letters to his brother Theo, written not 200 feet away. Our pilgrimage to San Remy-Provence has reached an anticipatory, but incomplete climax. Earlier in the morning we had silently slipped into the hospital cloister where the demon-tortured Vincent had admitted himself and roomed during the second to last year of his life. As Jay reads, our shade is intermittently interrupted by the wind. We are blinded by the sun, and Vincent speaks to us.

"My dear brother – I always write to you in between bouts of work, and I am working like one truly possessed, more than ever I am in the grip of a pent-up fury of work, and I'm sure it will help to cure me. Perhaps something along the lines of what Eugene Delacroix spoke of will happen to me – 'I discover painting when I had neither teeth nor breath left,' in the sense that my sad illness makes me work in a pent-up fury – very slowly – but without leaving off from morning till night – and – that is probably the secret – to work long and slowly. But what do I know about?"

Vincent produced a painting every day and a half for the remaining one and a half years of his life in a burst of creativity that probably has not been eclipsed by any other artist. If creativity is to be measured by today's market value per painting, he has no equal, and San Remy was the incubator of some of his most treasured works. If inspiration for creativity is our groups' quest, and it is, aside from Michaelangelo's Sistine Chapel, we couldn't have found a more hallowed place for our reflection.

From when our group first banded together, there has been a longing to squeeze from our molecules our most creative selves. Storytelling is one of our mediums, but not the exclusive agent. Meeting twice a year for four days and three nights since 1993, Jay and his partner Doug Lipman, storyteller, coach, and musician extraordinaire, have orchestrated a constant, overflowing, adult toy box of surprises that proves to our eager little band that we have never lost our childhood or our wondrous joy. We never knew how much our souls yearned for periodic diets of play, zany improvisational musicals, and sculpted stories from our childhood and reflected adulthood.

When we are together, with prompts from Jay and Doug, we zone into a world of creative expression, that is only fleetingly experienced in our daily lives. It is always the catalyst for a collective high. We are a rich and gutsy bouillabaisse formed from a collection of ten women and men, ranging in age from 35 to 65 who, if observed separately, would strike you as conscientious, well mannered, and certainly caring, but hardly artistic types. But, when we come together, we are 4th of July sparklers. The experience of the group taps into subterranean territory: play left in childhood, wackiness left in adolescence, and spontaneity atrophied during middle age.

Our group's pilgrimage to Van Gogh's Provence, was prompted by this history, plus a larger vision as well. How can we be more creative, and what's stopping us?

Our weekends together are always fun. They never come with heavy expectations of how-we-are-going-to-be-better-persons. We avoid pop-psychologizing. Oh, sure. We always seek to improve our stories and better shape their presentations. Performance is the object, not ourselves. But following Van Gogh's path to Southern France is a little different. We are on a soulful mission. Temporarily forsaking our professions, families, or a lazy sun-drenched beach vacation, we are on a quest to touch, grasp, and ultimately embrace that uniqueness which is ours, but buried under layers of prescriptions from others.

I thought, "If this is the measure for creativity, I'm in tough shape." I'm a product of a bourgeois household where my normalcy, some would say ordinariness, is a clear threat to unique expression. My Midwestern childhood home had no room for imaginative foolishness. Mom and Dad's message was: work hard, make good grades, mow the lawn, and make a good living after you leave home. There was no room for hurt, pain or self-pity. If you tripped or got dealt a bad hand, you got up and moved on. My closest encounter with pain had been a long separation and divorce and temporary separation from my two beloved daughters. Do you earn your right to be imaginative through suffering? Jay read excerpts from Van Gogh's letters to us most every morning. Vincent did not shirk from confronting his hurt.

"During the attacks, I feel cowardly in the face of the pain and suffering – more cowardly than is justified – and perhaps it is this moral cowardice itself, which previously I had no desire to cure, that now makes me eat for two, work hard, and limit my relations

with the other patients for fear of falling ill again – in short, I am trying to recover, like someone who has meant to commit suicide, but then makes for the bank because he finds the water too cold."

There it was: artistic product is correlated with the life pain of the artist. By this accounting: Van Gogh 100, Leader 1. Thanks a lot, Van Gogh! No pain, no artistic gain. I see myself as an imaginative teacher. Have I been less so because my pain quotient is relatively low? Or, is it as Van Gogh also suggested – it's not the pain, but what you do with it.

Here's my mentor, Jay O'Callahan with a global reputation as a storyteller, filling successful venues as far away as Australia, with over 50 taped stories and *Time Magazine* acclaiming him as "amazing," organizing a trip to hear the voice of Van Gogh, the oracle in the land of the artist's most productive years. What's the measure of Jay's creativity? Do you compare the sizes of audiences of Jay with Spaulding Grey? Do you compare the number of lines of laudatory newspaper copy? How much will people pay for a performance from each? What's the criteria? The pain index? Market value? Popularity? Van Gogh sold only two paintings during his life time.

When she came to Provence with us, Barbara (another member of our group), had to her credit a goodly number of published children's books.

Each of them rhymed, compelling the reader to enter a rich and articulated fantasy world. But she was not content with this record. There was more for her to give. Barbara had to be in motion, and the prompts came from a deep and soulful place, an unspoken cry to be witnessed and recognized for who she truly was.

Two summers ago, she had visited Provence, and with a borrowed dirt bike, explored the Luberon valley and mountains behind the inn where we were staying. Her stories of scaling the heights and being panicked by the foreboding caves below were part of the mysterious appeal that attracted us to Provence. Barbara's mission was to organize, map, and in many instances, guide bike and walking trips to the mountains. She became the mountain's high-priestess, challenging each of us to submit to the discipline of going beyond our practiced capabilities and experience the exhilaration of a new place in ourselves.

Rising to her challenge, on Wednesday afternoon I rode with Barbara and two others to complete a bike climb comparable to New Hampshire's White Mountains. I felt taxed, worn and stretched, but was ultimately successful. On Thursday, I was invited to be her companion on a duet pull that would out-distance anything that she or anyone in the group had achieved. The previous day's ride felt like my physiological limitations had been assaulted, raised, and were pegged at their outer boundaries. But I could not deny Barbara's proposal, even though there was a disturbing internal message that I was risking, at some level, my mortality. Her invitation was to literally and figuratively reconfigure my head and heart; a new constellation in my thinking was required.

The peddling commenced. Revisiting yesterday's apex was painful with shortened breath, tingling calves, and aching hands, but it didn't scare me. I was white-knuckled when we stopped for water. The next 50 minutes was a harmonious syncopation of my pumping feet and Barbara's assuring and soothing word spells that inoculated me from any stray thoughts that I wouldn't make it.

We were approaching the summit when Barbara, ahead of me, cautioned, "Stay to your right!"

Raising my eyes from the pavement, I was accosted by the vision of a pack of helmeted, rainbow-clad cyclists, hurling towards me like guided missiles on a trajectory that wouldn't miss its mark. Initially startled, but not disarmed, I steered off their course. My awkwardly executed but functionally complete maneuver was a compliment to Barbara's studied and creative skills as a cycling coach and a capstone for me of creativity on demand.

On our first day together, Jay had given us the assignment to find a character in the town marketplace, study him or her, and bring the experience back with us. It was mid-morning, and nothing had invaded my consciousness, when a lady in red literally swept in front of me, broom in hand. Perhaps it was the incongruity that alerted my eye: the obvious presentation dress, layered with gauzy red and yellow taffeta and carefully colored hair juxtaposed with her swinging broom. After a needless and nervous sweep of the tiny front porch of her antique shop, featuring canvases of anthropomorphized canines, she slid herself into a waiting lawn chair and proceeded to give a mime performance that could best be appreciated by readers of a 1950s French fashion magazine. The staging certainly was not for the current customers going in and out of the gallery, to which she was almost completely oblivious, nor even to those who greeted her with a "bonjour." She was so fascinated by her own performance, that I didn't interrupt it when I was only seven feet away. So creative was her one act play, and done without any apparent reward, audience, or incentive, that I could only give its rightful due by being an understudy of its enactment and performing it for my storytelling group.

My hands mimicked hers, in constant motion, at once soothing the face, then smoothing and replacing errant hairs in the carefully combed French twist. Remembering the subtleties of motion of her quickly moving fingers, I patted and stroked my and her 60-year-old skin back to the sculpted form of a 20-year-old. My legs tangled seductively, stretching and re-curling, forcing a realignment of my fantasized dress to allow just a little more exposure of the thigh. Periodically, I pressed down on a button dial of an imaginary phone for an animated and humor-provoked conversation, while at the same time reshaping my eyebrows with my little finger, just before giving a devilish wink from a side-casting eye.

I was the lady in red, and I could feel her pain. It came from a deep well of hurt, an incomplete life, a grasping for attention that was no longer forthcoming; maybe it never had been. Her and my performance didn't need an audience. Didn't warrant an admission price. It was enough just to be.

Theo wrote to Vincent in 1889 that his paintings had been positively reviewed by one of Paris's leading critics and enclosed a copy for Vincent's inspection. Vincent's reply was appreciative, but he seemed unmoved by the recognition.

"Now I content myself with the thought that by working diligently one may perhaps make some progress even without thinking about it … I should like to do portraits which would appear as revelations to people in a hundred years' time."

INUIT PASSAGE – ARCTIC CHALLENGES

THERE ARE WHITECAPS FROM A thirty-knot wind beating against a receding tide. They are pounding our minivan-sized open boat. The hugely underpowered outboard motor is losing the battle. Jimmy Grist, at least 70 years old, has clearly transcended any sense of fear and stands down the wind at his makeshift, weather-beaten, plywood helm with his month-long beard, gnarled face, and stringy, white hair glorifying in the tough gusts.

He appears oblivious to the shudders that the canoe-shaped boat experiences as it meets every water slap. We're on a water buffalo repeatedly trying to dislodge its cargo of Lucy, Wren, his buddy Sand, and me, who are huddled, cross-legged, in its bowels. The bucking crescendos, and we are white-knuckled, faces smeared with sea foam and mouths spitting salt water, anticipating the final vertical leap which will cast us, as so many offerings, to the waiting river. One stroke, I morbidly calculate, will move our place from the highest position to the lowest on nature's food chain.

"How much further?" I yell my inquiry, wanting to be heard without letting on how terrified I am, while remaining respectful of his captain's status.

No response; he doesn't hear me. Jimmy is occupied with his own thoughts: *If they want to go fishing, I'll take them. It's not the time, I keep telling them, it's mid-August and the salmon bellies are full, and they are not interested in phony lures. They've gone up to the rapids, getting ready to spawn. We'll high-tail after them. If these crazy Americans want to fish, by God, we'll fish. If it's salmon they want, they shall have salmon.*

How in the hell did I risk my family and myself in this remote stretch of the planet? We are on the Koksoak tidal river in Quebec's northern-most region, roughly 55-degree latitude, the same latitude as Anchorage, Alaska, but we're due north of Montreal.

What is Jimmy trying to do? I'm fairly certain he doesn't want to kill us. Then it dawns on me, in this moment of panic where in retrospect events unfold like a grainy, black and white, 8-millimeter home movie. He's just trying to please us. Yes, he's trying to please us. He's been trying to please us ever since we showed up on his radar two days earlier.

That's it: the critical piece in the puzzle. Jimmy didn't want to go fishing this Saturday morning. The freighter canoe, as the Inuit call them, hadn't tasted water for three years and was quite content to stay land-bound for another three. It was 8 AM when we arrived, having made arrangements with Jimmy yesterday afternoon. In fact, it's the last thing he wanted to do; his wife, burdened with Alzheimer's, wanders around the house and needs his attention. We came to Jimmy because everyone we met said he was one of the best salmon fishermen, and we told him so. Jimmy wasn't going to let us down. Besides, the four of us were staying with his brother-in-law and had to be taken care of. It's what you do for family.

For weeks I was wondering if going on that arctic oceanic sojourn was the best thing I could do for my family. However, Jimmy's apocalyptic canoe ride was the catalyst to begin to unravel the mystery tour the four of us had been on for the five previous days. Kuujjuaq had treated us, not as tourists, but as if we were royalty, and they had not previously known us from Adam. What's more, they weren't interested in our money. This non-commercial, pleasing attitude threw me off. It was there from the start.

Cruise North's expedition to the Arctic didn't garner more than three sentences in a brief piece on native North American-sponsored travel in the *Boston Globe* last winter. But that it was organized and run by Inuits, offered kayaking in waters teeming with whales, and that summer would avail tourists of their pilot efforts, aroused our family's sense of adventure. This might take its place alongside camping in Tanzania and touring Southern India in the monsoon season.

The Arctic pulled me. But a ship expedition was not going to be enough. We took on five, unplanned days, in Kuujjuaq to meet Inuits before sailing. The Inuit, who people the northern polar circumference from Russia to Alaska, have a compelling history. For example, during the Middle Ages, these Indigenous people were able to adapt to a dramatic drop in temperature while Westerners could not. In Greenland, the agriculturally-minded Norse could not adjust to the longer winters, while the Inuits continued to thrive as they shifted from a nomadic existence to fishing and hunting caribou.

Severe climactic change is still a threat to the Innuits, compounded by our First World societies' insatiable appetite for pelts, land, oil, and antlers, not to speak of adventure. We are gifted in trampling over Indigenous people. What have we done to the Inuit, and how are they surviving? I had hoped to discover the answers to these questions on this journey.

Kuujjuaq, a village of 2,800 is the largest settlement and center of government of a territory known as Nunavik, the northernmost landmass of Quebec, defined by Hudson Bay on its western shore and Hudson's Straight on the east. The majority of this land is deeded to the Indigenous Inuit population by the province of Quebec and the Canadian government. The government didn't give it away however; the Inuit took them to court in 1975 when Quebec was posturing to devastate their salmon, trout, and Arctic char streams with enormous hydro-dams.

The Inuit now govern themselves and have wisely invested money paid to them for land still owned by Canada and Quebec. Civic and social services, health care, schools, and internet access for all of Nunavik's twelve villages, have been their first priority. Of equal importance to their economy's long-term viability have been funds set aside to support entrepreneurial ventures to relieve dependence on hunting and fishing, a form of livelihood which has become increasingly more problematic with the acceleration of global warming. The ventures have been as diverse as operating airlines, roasting coffee, producing designer-line fur fashion, and making caribou pate.

Kuujjuaq, currently a robust center of commerce, has had a precarious history. The indigenous people had encampments on the river probably for millennia, where fishing and hunting was bountiful. Yearly, tens of thousands of caribou made treks through the region. Polar bears, seals, and walrus were 10 miles downriver. It was white men who gave Kuujjuaq a place on the global map, but the price was upending their traditional hunting and fishing economy into a commercial marketplace.

Henry Hudson, in 1600, was the first to upset the delicate balance between Inuit and nature. It was Henry who put Hudson Bay on the world map, that in turn, drew the Hudson Bay Company, which traded western goods for pelts, forever changing Inuit life. From an Inuit perspective, it was true justice when Hudson, on his fourth voyage to North America to find the elusive Northwest Passage, was set adrift with his son by his mutinous crew at the bottom of the bay ultimately named for him, never to be heard from again. Henry could charm London investors, but he couldn't lead. He was done in by the same man and compatriots who had tried three times earlier on three previous voyages, and who finally pulled off a successful mutiny - an ignoble ending to a most un-heroic explorer. Without Henry, there would be no Hudson Bay and no Hudson Bay Company and no knowledge of Kuujjuaq.

Let me take you back to when we stepped off our Air Inuit flight from Montreal to Kuujjuaq. We felt as naïve but expectant as Dorothy did in *Oz*.

The passenger manifest was brimming with dark and light-skinned, round-faced Inuits with shy and narrow, lively eyes. Their wide foreheads and appealing smiles announced a distinct presence. The baby and kid count equaled the number of adults. Awaiting their arrival was an equal, if not greater, number of relatives and friends. We greet family and close friends with discreet hugs and smiles, but their celebration was palpable, punctuated with yelps of joy. These were people who truly prized being with one another.

The other passengers on the plane were men from "the South," as the literally-worded Inuits labeled anyone not of their blood. They came decked out in camouflage parkas and pants, and once their baggage was unloaded, they were quick to check out their rifles with polished stocks and gleaming barrels. They were clearly headed for men-only good times. Their repartee was filled with one-liners and one-upmanship. "Whoa, George, what you carryin'? Looks like a bazooka. Are you going for a big one this year? Last year's wasn't much off the tits. Be careful, there might be nothin' left using that iron."

The ever-solicitous Inuit drivers for the hunting camps stacked enormous quantities of Budweiser on double-cabbed, all-wheel-drive pickups. It looked as if they were ready for big game trophies. It was only later that I learned there wasn't much sport in shooting gallery-style: picking off listless caribou who collaborated in their own demise by lining up and strolling on the same yearly trails to their winter birthing grounds. Racks of caribou antlers would soon festoon game rooms "down South" that would resound with accounts of the great hunt. The rest of the caribou were left for the Inuits who knew exactly how to fashion every piece of the remaining carcass into something useful. They produced clothing, bedding, and bags, from its skin and tools and weapons from its bones. Noting that fats in the caribou leg joints congealed at lower temperatures the farther they were from the body core, they took the fat from the feet to use as a lubricant for bow strings in freezing temperatures.

We were temporarily left isolated and standing alone between two cultures who met and conducted their prearranged, mutual business. But neither one would touch each other personally. The hunters would see to that. They were interested in antlers, not Inuits.

Each of our fellow passengers had somebody to greet them. The four of us were standing, bags in hand, with no accommodations, with nothing planned for five days, in an Inuit village which was precariously placed on a barren landscape of permafrost. All this on the veracity of Richard Jones' word, our self-appointed ambassador, who we had never met.

Richard, the village fire chief, true to his word that he would see to our visit, eventually arrived. It would be Richard and the village elders who would unlock the community for us to witness: its exuberance for life, its entrepreneurial achievements, and the social dependence for those whom the modern world was too much.

With our gear stored in the fire chief's Ford SUV, Richard said we were off to the home of Norman Ford, a retired tugboat captain. After we had decided to visit Kuujjuaq, we phoned, seeking accommodations, only to be told by one hotel that it was too expensive, and the other said that it had the only bar in town, and we would, as a family, find it too smoky and rowdy. At first, it seemed they didn't want us to come. One person asked, "Why would you ever want to come to Kuujjuaq?" But underneath the question, they were saying, "We are honored by you just coming to be with us. You can become part of our community."

Kuujjuaq unfolded before us. Neat, wooden, rectangular boxes the size of double railroad boxcars lined the streets. The houses were painted with primary colors from windowsills up. Each was suspended two or three feet off the ground by industrial strength, automotive-like jacks, which were adjusted after the spring thaw to level the structure on the fickle-surfaced permafrost. Each house was self-contained with tanks for water, heating oil, and disposable waste, serviced by a fleet of roaming trucks that pumped and extracted the houses' life fluids, but remained connected via phone and internet. From the air, it resembled a child's toy village of brightly-colored blocks, unencumbered by not one neon or painted sign of commercial life.

I was shocked. The reality of Kuujjuaq didn't fit my expectations, admittedly, woefully out of date. My vision had been as frozen as the Arctic icecap is in winter. Robert Flaherty's film, *Nanuk of the North*, which I had seen in high school, invaded my consciousness not to be disturbed until my arrival in Kuujacq. The film conveyed the Arctic as a desolate, forbidding landscape (a frozen version of our wild, wild West), where, as interpreted by Flaherty (a Westerner with Inuit blood), only the heroic endure. Nanuk's family is on the verge of starvation and he saves it by: finding a golf ball-hole-sized opening in the ice, harpooning a creature below the surface, and then going through a Chaplinesque tug-of-war with it. The line goes in and out, and Nanuk tumbles, pulls, and jerks. Finally, with the help of his family, they yank a black, Loch-Ness-sized, tubular, seal from the opening. It is sliced and diced, followed by scenes of the extended family gnawing at and feasting on the seal blubber. This was an Arctic encounter with a primitive food-chain battle between man and sea mammal. This was something more than sport; this was survival, each making the other more heroic.

Clearly now, Kuujjuaq was a very different place. Norman Ford greeted us as if we were long-lost cousins, just as Richard had earlier at the airport. It was disarming. It felt undeserved. But it was the treatment we received on our first phone encounter, and it continued unabated throughout our stay.

Norman's home screamed: "missing mom." The refrigerator was sparingly populated with leftover takeout. Neat piles of laundered clothing, rolled up rugs, and camping gear punctuated the sparsely-furnished, bare-floored, four-bedroom house. Hotpoint and Maytag appliances, as well as a large TV and stereo console were surprisingly prominent features of the household. No igloo here. We had been apprised by Richard that Norman's wife had died three years earlier, leaving their adopted teenage son, Arthur, for Norman to raise, while the younger, adopted daughter was being raised by Arthur's sister in a nearby village. Arthur was never around. He was trusted to be independent, and the rest was left to the community.

Norman needed, at least temporarily, a replacement family, and we were it. Lucy cooked, and we shared meals family-style. In keeping with our presumed family-like status, Norman pressed the keys to his recently-washed and polished red Ford pickup into my hand and told me we would need it to get around. The risk of strangers driving off with the truck was mitigated by the fact that there were no roads out of town.

The twelve villages of Nunavik were connected by water in the summer and only by air in the winter.

Richard and Norman were early, and it turned out, long-term runners in a social relay race, where we became the baton in an unplanned, yet culturally-orchestrated race to incorporate us into their community. Jimmy Grist, our erstwhile boat helmsman, was simply playing his part in our incorporation.

The relay went as follows: from Richard to Norman to Jimmy and then to Allen, who would see to our helicopter ride with Peter. Peter would slip us into an excursion within his business of transferring enormous drilling bits between oil pumping platforms.

Peter also kept track of the wandering musk oxen herds. We were privileged to witness these Jurassic cattle who had not made one evolutionary step in several hundred millennia. With several layers of insulating wool, like so many dirty bathmats piled on one another and tiny Fred-Astaire-hoofed feet poking through at the bottom, these so endowed mammals do not require shelter in the most extreme Arctic weather. They have been known to survive minus eighty degrees Fahrenheit with seventy-five mile-per-hour headwinds, winds that would submerge the windchill to only laboratory-induced levels of cold.

Here is the stark recollection of our time with Peter: we were but twenty feet off the permafrost, suspended in mid-air, in our whirling capsule. Giant, spongy earphones are pasted on our ears with straw-like microphones wrapped to our mouths.

"At 11 o'clock, you can just see a herd forming. I'll keep a distance. We don't want to scare them," Peter said.

"Roger, are they making a circle?" I asked.

"As you would say in the states, they're circling the wagon. The one out front pawing around, he's the chief. He's ready to do battle."

The evolutionary adaptation displayed by Peter juxtaposed with the stagnant musk oxen was overwhelming. Our Inuit pilot's ancestors had hunted these large, relatively inert mammals on this very land which was currently their preserve. The musk oxen are now an endangered species. Their failure to trade up their DNA status is protected by the benevolence of a society which did. Peter's Inuit community had seen to his education, pilot training, and seed money for his helicopter business.

Between two harrowing river experiences, was the similarly high-energy Aqpik Jam Music Festival. We attended three successive nights, and it spoke both to Nunavik's capacity for fun and enjoyment of life, as well as to the price the community was paying for tasting the spectrum of first-world treats. This was an annual gathering of the clan from all twelve villages. Those who could catch a boat ride, hoist a teepee, or garner floor space for sleeping with a relative were present.

People of all ages came to enjoy themselves: tug-of-war and games in the morning before barbequed salmon, freshly-killed, raw seal blubber, burgers, and hot dogs at noon, and a cacophony of music and fireworks at night. It was the opportunity to attend this music jam that helped entice Wren and Sand to be equally invested in this Arctic adventure. Though the musicianship and music of the accordion-playing and throat-singing locals wasn't close to a 30,000-strong Springsteen get-down, for the first two nights, the audience reception and enthusiasm may have exceeded anything that The Boss has received.

Kuujjuaq's Tom-Cruise-handsome Mayor and his equally young and able town officials produced and paid for the whole show with town funds. On the last night, the community's year-long, stored-up, rectitude was going to have an orgasmic release to rival Rio and New Orleans' Mardi Gras. This was to be Alcoholics Anonymous, Kuujjuaq-style.

The 300-seat auditorium-style village community center, merely three years old, adorned with the latest electronics and acoustic gear, played out its designated role in the celebration. Its walls pulsated and throbbed, propelled by a twelve-piece rock band, whose agonized, on-stage contortions were, rather surprisingly, utterly useless in arousing the audience's attention. The band might not have been there as far as they were concerned. The assembled were too busy systematically getting ripped. On this final night of the festival, any genetically-blooded Inuit could stand in line to receive a back-of-the-hand stamp signifying a non-alcohol abuser, and then join another line where he or she could purchase two cans of beer at a time, with six refills assumed and fully-utilized.

Starting at 5 PM, a line of silent, blank-faced, almost zombie-like men and women snaked through the Center's foyer and outside, ready to receive their admission to the community-sanctioned and alcohol-assisted bash. By 9 PM, the place was bouncing with shrieks of laughter, wobbly attempts at dancing, and off-key serenades. Everybody was having a good time, but I felt shocked. The scene was surreal. Like a grade B movie version of Cinderella: a big party, but this time, the bacchanal extended to the wee hours of the morning, and then the revelers returned to their unadorned, rectangular, pre-fab homes for the rest of the year.

However, I noticed something that confused me. None of the community leaders who had orchestrated our visit got hammered. Norman Foster, our housing host, there with his buddies, toasted in moderation. Allen had sold raffle tickets for a Singer sewing machine to attract customers to his wife's business. The mayor, in between introducing the musical acts, busied himself with the sound system. Richard, the fire chief, and Peter, our helicopter pilot, and their wives were nowhere to be seen.

Then it hit me. Kuujjuaq was a two-class society: those who manage and those who *are* managed. This was my first exposure to the latter, having been passed around by the managers, who were *locus parenti* for those whom modernity was too much. Alcoholism, family abuse, listlessness, and dependency on welfare were the underbelly of a community that had the surface appearance of a utopia. Those in the community who took advantage of western technology, rather than being simply the recipients of its treats, stepped in and banned the retail sale of alcohol in Kuujjuaq when it threatened to overwhelm the community. Of course, waging a zero-tolerance alcohol consumption policy was impossible. It hadn't been eradicated. It was just more expensive and difficult to purchase.

But the seduction of drink can't be the only problem that challenges a coming-of-age Inuit. Why do some make it and others don't? Is there a secret for success? It took a boat trip around the Nunavik coastline to come up with some amateur explanations.

When I spied the squat, converted National Oceanographic and Atmospheric Association research vessel, it didn't seem up to the 1,500 nautical mile trip. The ship looked like a bobbing toy boat in a giant bathtub of a river, which had scared the hell out of us earlier in the week. That aquatic experience was merely the tune-up for the ferocity of Hudson's Straight, which had confounded mariners for centuries with a 25-mile-wide avalanche of water, which we would take straight-on. My confidence in the excursion was waning even before I was on board.

Then, too, the ship came with a tension-inducing history. Although a veteran workhorse for plying the ice fields of

Antarctica, the ship and its South American crew seemed ill-adapted to the Arctic. The expedition prior to ours had to be abandoned and the passengers sent home when the ship went aground in the river, at about the same place where it was now anchored. The Argentinean Captain was fired because he wouldn't trust the word of the native Inuit river guide who came aboard to pilot the ship up the river to Kuujjuaq. What the Captain perceived as bad advice as to when, where, and how the ship should anchor, turned out to be his undoing. Pig-headedness doesn't compute well with those who stay close to nature's currents. We were to have a new captain, but the fact of his inexperience was not calming.

While the Inuit had organized the expedition, they had subcontracted the ship and its crew and the leadership to professional tour guides from the US who had earned their polar stripes on tours to the Antarctic — that is, save for Jessie and Bruce. These two short, stockily-built, mid-20s, full-blooded Inuits were our designated culture and nature guides. She, politically savvy, with a constant knowing, twinkling smile, and he, persistently anxious from carrying a burden of unaccustomed responsibility. It was a Linus and Lucy pairing that made them so effective as a team.

One afternoon, the two introduced Inuit games which put a premium on physical agility and strength. Sand was the only volunteer, and he equaled the standards set by Bruce but was clearly overpowered and outmaneuvered by Jessie in a leg wrestle. She flipped him upside-down with one powerful stroke. This was her second win over a male. She had done the same with Bruce a few minutes earlier. By the trip's end, however, Sand had earned a special place with Bruce and Jessie.

Frequently, the two did the spotting when the ship was underway, while the Caucasian did the announcing. "Look ahead on your starboard side. An iceberg floating this way with three ring seals…OK, now two. Be quick, there goes another. Those of you on the stern should have a good camera angle for the little baby seal."

Jessie fulfilled her cultural guide role with PowerPoint-slide-assisted talks about her people, using her own life as an example. She was born and raised on the land where her family was dependent upon hunting and fishing for their housing, food, and clothing, with a meager amount left over to barter for what they couldn't use or eat themselves. She was one of ten sibling girls and a brother, who she subsequently learned, after leaving home, was a cousin taken in by Jessie's parents when her aunt couldn't take care of him. The revelation was of little consequence. Her and the Inuit's idea of family had permeable boundaries as to who was included. Jessie, as of August, 2005, had 135 first cousins and still counting.

Inuit familial ties, either by blood or marriage, unequivocally qualify one as being included in a bonded community. But could others be so accepted? And how? We were so blessed by our reception in Kuujjuaq. What did we unknowingly do to gain admission? What keeps others out? Living, even for a short time, with a culture so foreign to my own stimulated my anthropological curiosity.

Jessie and Bruce diligently executed their nature and cultural guide responsibilities, but they also left a trail of subtle openings for engaging with them beyond their formalized roles. Cues were dropped, and how they were picked up was decisive in establishing a different relationship with them. The Q & A following a session prompted another shipboard traveler to ask, "Jessie, you've had a number of responsible jobs. What is the percentage of Inuit going to college?" Another posed the question, "I've read alcoholism is a big problem with the Inuit. How are you dealing with it?"

Lucy, on the other hand, listened and responded to Jessie as a woman whose own life passage had parallels to those of Jessie: an early, ill-fated marriage, a feminist perspective, filled with persistent independence. Lucy treated Jessie as an educator and not as a curiosity. She honored Jessie by respecting her talents. The character of their relationship was announced to those who attended Jessie's second shipboard lecture, when Lucy was introduced as "my ship mother." This was in keeping with the Inuit's literal naming practices, but saved for those who took a genuine interest in their humanity. By the expedition's end, Wren, Sand, and I had been included in Jessie's inventory. We were advertised as her "ship family."

Jessie was on our trip because she had broken out of her subsistence background but never abandoned it. She had a year of college in Montreal, accounting experience at a local government agency, a modeling contract, and was the culture guide for Cruise North, but she kept one foot firmly planted in her family's ancestral wilderness camp. Her yearly retreats there served a functional family need: she parented, cooked, and sewed. But it was also a condition of her self-image.

When Jessie casually mentioned that in the fall she would be taking her kids to Toronto for a fashion photography shoot, I finally got it. What distinguished Jessie, Bruce, Allen, Peter, Richard, and Norman from their local brothers and sisters was their capacity and desire to live in two very different worlds: one part in their cherished Inuit heritage and the other as robust citizens of a global economy. We had flown over Peter's camp. Allen was reintroducing, with a U.S. partner, a team of purebred Inuit sled dogs for a tourist market, and Norman was patiently building an aluminum igloo in his backyard to house snowmobiles to travel to his winter hunting camp. Clearly, these people wouldn't give up one world for the other. The tension between the two worlds gave them energy, sanctuary, and identity.

Jessie caught me at midpoint in my Inuit cultural immersion. Bruce unexpectedly finished the job. Shy in demeanor with little or no social conversational skills, his perpetually tense face telegraphed the burden of his shipboard responsibilities. They clearly weighed heavily on him. Something unexpected, maybe disastrous, always seemed around the corner for Bruce.

On our shore expeditions to locate polar bear and musk oxen, Bruce, wore a high-caliber rifle, snug between his back and right shoulder blade. It was for protection, not hunting, as he led those of us venturing forth from the safety of the ship. Most of the time we couldn't keep up with his pace, which clearly frustrated him. Though our Caucasian tour guides clearly saw themselves as wildlife-competent and in-charge, it always seemed to work out that Bruce ended up as the point person on our shore forays. His status was no accident. It was Bruce who faced down, with feigned belligerence, a polar bear stalking our beached Zodiac landing craft. The wily bear, lumbered away, knowing he had met his match, and our party's flesh and provisions were not for the taking.

Our final Arctic challenge was accepted by only Sand and me. Everyone else left to visit a nearby Inuit village. Bruce outfitted Sand with his kayak and then shoehorned me into my own sliver of an ocean kayak. He buttoned to it a canvas skirt that surrounded my waist, designed to keep water out should I encounter rocky seas. There's little room inside for even air, let alone H2O. My heart pounded as Bruce shoved a paddle into my purple, cold hands, and launched me into the Northern-most point of Hudson's Bay.

The first two or three strokes of my double-ended oar were fine. Then abruptly, I rolled side-to-side in my half-moon shaped kayak. A sudden pitch had me at forty-five degrees before I recovered with a paddle thrust - only lasting a second, but long enough to fully appreciate the forty-degree water. The palatable hot blood coursing through my veins ignited an old tape: the scene was all wrong. Something was amiss. I signed up for our trip north in order to kayak in the Arctic. I fantasized stroking among glistening, sunlit icebergs in pristine waters, occasionally punctuated by ripples from a breaching beluga whale. But now I felt like I was upon a water tight-rope, barely able to steady myself. Luckily it got a little better as I stroked forward and regained my balance. Alas, the waves picked up, and I teetered. I've ocean kayaked many times. What was I doing wrong? There must be a technique that I was missing.

I wanted to call out, but Bruce and Sand were nowhere in sight. I was alone. At that moment, I was overcome by an image of myself upside-down in the water, immobilized by the tethered kayak, with tiny bubbles peacefully trailing to the surface. All motion was suspended, but the effect was counterintuitive: I felt cleansed and at peace. My anxiety washed away, and I felt at one with the water. I increased my stroke with renewed energy.

With eerie timing, Bruce approached me, hailing me from my stern. "You are fine. I have family in the village. You be back by 3."

And I did make it back, having viewed a sizable sea mammal that crossed my path. I will never know, because I don't want to know, whether or not my particular introduction by Bruce to Arctic sea-kayaking was planned or fortuitous. I did learn, however, that you don't talk about these matters. Yet I have read Inuit children's stories and myths that are riddled with horrific tales demanding extraordinary resolution, fear that must be transcended by an equal proportion of courage. They, as a people, haven't survived without a healthy respect for a highly-unpredictable and harsh environment and a food supply that could vanish at any moment. It makes me wonder whether they may be better-prepared for global warming than the rest of the world.

A Love Letter to France

I DON'T KNOW WHEN IT FIRST struck me. Maybe it was the accumulation of several episodes on my two-week holiday in July, but I've come to the conclusion that France is an endangered First World culture and needs global protection.

First, to set the matter straight, I came away from my first visit to France as a Francophile phobic. It was in 1959, and my first wife Joan and I were driving a VW bug rented in Germany on our first tour of Europe. We landed in Paris late one night, exhausted, and took a tiny room in a 5th floor walk-up on the Left Bank.

At three in the morning, three gendarmes in full police regalia burst into our room, treating Joan as if she were an unlicensed lady of the night and me, her john. The pretext for this harassment was patently transparent when the demand in French to see our passports, having not been understood by us, was given emphasis in pigeon German. Of course, there were profuse apologies when our true identifies were established, but that didn't mollify us much, when the next morning we found our Beetle with two broken windows and all possessions missing.

Subsequently, a romantic visit with Lucy to Giverny where Monet painted (with inspired vigor well into his 80's), the water lilies, global icons of what is great art, and then several interludes staying at small hotels on Isle St. Louis (along with luxuriously delectable meals), have done much to erase my initial impression of France. Still, I have never found the French receptive to my inability to speak their language. Unlike Italians, where language is not a prerequisite to hospitality, Parisians, in particular, always seemed demonstrably annoyed that I could not speak French and by facial gesture, speak it well.

But this time around, either I came with a new attitude or France had changed or both. The first day in Paris inspired a revelation that didn't dissipate during my visit. Lucy, Wren and I were enjoying lunch with her brother, Ken and sister-in-law, Eunice, at Café Marley in sight of the Louvre, engrossed in I.M. Pei's luminous three-story-high glass pyramid penetrating the museum courtyard. The ornate 15th century building, which houses the museum, was the backdrop to this artistic violation. Even though the museum was closed, you wouldn't know it. The courtyard was filled with people, perhaps mistakenly drawn because they thought the museum was open, but now captured by the beauty of taking in and being a part of this aesthetic experience.

Following lunch, we strolled through the adjacent garden of the Palais-Royale where a 100-yard allée of Linden trees, mature cousins of those surrounding the Christian Science Center's reflecting pool in Boston, provided a cool retreat from the afternoon sun. On one side of this dark allée, a temporary outdoor sculpture installation by Polish artist, Magdalena Abakanowicz commanded our attention. A death chorus of headless, rusted metal, Holocaust victims would not let us proceed until we had contemplated the meaning of that event.

This complexity of visual stimulation and reflection continued when we chanced upon a pulsating and extravagant fountain in a large circular pool, fizzing momentary rainbows as the wind shifted direction. It was crowded. The steel green park chairs of Paris, ubiquitous as pigeons in New York, played siege to the pond, peopled by embracing couples worthy of Cartier-Bresson exposures. Singletons were intensely absorbed in their books and newspapers.

I felt an almost irresistible desire to participate, to linger and take part in this homage to pleasure. But I was divided. The American side of me told me to relinquish this "non-productive" activity and to do and see more of Paris.

Maybe it wasn't right there and then; it probably took several leisurely meals, punctuated by a variety of refined and complex wines and cheeses, for the realization to firmly take hold, but there was a growing awareness that my personal dilemma at the fountain in the park of Palais-Royale was divided between the cultures of the U.S. and France. We derive our satisfaction from different stimuli and different synapses in our psyches.

In a mere five Parisian hours, my senses were aglow, tickled and caressed. How could this be? Clearly, the pace of the day, languid and destination-less, had something to do with it. It allowed me to absorb the bath of sensory stimulation surrounding me. A day in the U.S., even a holiday one, would be a race against an imaginary score card, checking off how many museums, parks, and great meals had been seen, walked, and eaten.

The alternative French experience is conveniently captured by a country comparison of the number of cafés and their outdoor chairs, with accompanying waiters, per urban square mile. You can't walk a block in Paris, and for that matter - in Arles, Nimes or any other French city - without having a basserie on either end, each with enough seating for The Tabernacle Choir. The classic 30-inch round French café table is primarily for schmoozing, gazing, and reading and only secondarily for eating. The economics of this space utilization would never pass muster in the U.S.

What does a 9-French Franc ($1.50) lemonade buy for you in the Franz Liszt Square in the 10th arrondissement of Paris? It bought me an outdoor chair overlooking a well-groomed park and a 17th Century cathedral with a classically inspired facade and enough statuary to satisfy any small museum. I had this seat for a good four, going on five hours, and, if I wanted it, for the day, with no questions asked. Not once did the waiter ask me (as would be the case in the U.S.), "Will there be anything more?" with the obvious implication that I better get eating or get out. No, I was free to partake of this visually crafted piece of the planet for the day for the price of a non-alcoholic drink.

And here is the embarrassing part of my story. What did I find myself pondering in the first hour of my seating: I was caught up in a prototypical American entrepreneurial daydream. Why did they allow the parked motor scooters and cycles to occupy so much space immediately adjacent to the outdoor tables and chairs? Couldn't they be directed to less commercially valuable space? And, why not have a per person minimum? It was ridiculous. People lingering for hours with, at most, a 30-Franc ($5.00) bill.

And there it was again. I found myself imposing my culture (where making my next dollar on my turf, albeit a geographic or cyber portal, is my bottom line), on a culture where space, while individually deeded or under government stewardship, is to be enjoyed by the collective. For example, Paris is a very clean city and it must be very expensive to keep it that way. An army of apple-green uniformed maintenance workers with matching reflective vests invade the city at dusk with determination that would be terrifying, if not immediately obvious, that expunging waste was their objective. Sweeping the sidewalks and streets and, at a trot, tipping waste barrels into slow moving, gigantic and spotless garbage haulers, they are Paris' gift to our visual and euphoric senses, not to speak of our compulsive sensibilities.

What was creeping up on me was that the French, compared to us, had a very different sense of not only space and what and whom it was for, but time as well. The abundance of chairs at any one cafe, the extravagant number of cafes, parks and museums compared to other cities of the world is telling. They wouldn't be there, if there weren't Parisians with time to populate them. Where and how the French spend their time and the daily rhythm of it divides our worlds more than the Atlantic.

This was illustrated by our visit to Parc de la Villette and their extraordinary Museum of Science and Industry, the largest and most extensive in Europe. At Wren's suggestion, I accompanied him to the automotive exhibit. This was not just about gearboxes, pistons and Peugeots of the 1930's. No, you were first ushered down a ramp alongside individual, futuristic video viewing booths, screening clips on the topic of cars. The first one set the tone; the subject was speed: how man had relentlessly competed to make racers go faster and faster over the century.

However, there was a difference from what would be expected from Detroit. The opening shot was a chetah running at full tilt after an ill-fated gazelle. The voice-over, reminded the viewer that in contrast to man, other species had a functional need for speed, that is, to sustain themselves. Why was man engaged in this pell-mell, headlong rush to go faster and faster? What was the point? Just to make sure the point was not lost, superimposed on the left side of the picture was a small-time clock, ticking away the elapsed time and with periodic verbal reminders on the time remaining. You literally were made to feel the pressure of time ticking away, that is, if you bought into the notion that your time was so precious.

The cultivation of the senses and the intellect to take precedence over the drive to accumulate, grow and succeed… and where to derive satisfaction – Americans may want to take a lesson from the French on this aspect of life to enhance our own *joie de vivre*.

Reed and Lois Foster – Bold Lives

Scene One. The Harvard Business School. October 1959. Reed Foster and I are in the Harvard Business School, Class of 1961. In the elite capitalistic boot camp, we prepare to outsmart our competitors in the business world. The arena is an enormous, multi-tiered classroom where 85 young males are locked in verbal jousting. We thrust and parry, as we attempt to gain the attention of the instructor and our classmates, winning recognition points for the analytic depth of our arguments and the polish of our verbal acuity.

Engaged in learning the case method, the discussions can range from the esoteric, such as Bayesian inference theory, to the mundane, "What should be this year's name for the color red on Ford's next model?" The pedagogical message is clear. Analyze the company's problems, take it down to its bare bones essentials, identify the critical mistakes of the past, and reassemble a plan for maximum profitability. There were no social responsibility fillets blocking this headlong goal.

Reed and I are only marginally in the classroom game; we're outsiders, observers, certainly not part of the inner core. We are both intimidated by the apparent savvy and competence of our classmates, fresh from Ivy League schools, some even with Wall Street experience. (Years later, Reed admitted, "I was in semi-shock both years of my degree. I was astonished at how articulate and aggressive those guys were. They had no fear whatsoever. I didn't think they were smarter than I was, I just didn't put myself in their same category.")

Our classroom experience was an amazing replication of and preparation for what we would encounter when we graduated. It was capitalism full tilt. The economy was expanding after the Korean War and the nation's self doubt in the late '60s, induced by the Vietnam War, was yet to come. We were solitary knights, about to fight our way to the top by outwitting our less-skilled competitors. You chose your colleagues carefully; the best were like yourself: same breeding, same boarding schools, same college. You chose wisely, because today's colleagues could be tomorrow's competitors. There was room for only one hand on the brass ring.

The Harvard Business School didn't accept female students in 1959. The only women on campus besides secretaries were wives and wives-to-be and only for social events on weekends. It's not as if they were devalued, it's that their value lay in being essential accessories to the corporate success of their male companions. In the battle for executive positions, absolute prerequisites were: an adoring spouse, a full-time mom, and a charming hostess. Lady Guinevere equivalents to the Crusaders of Yore.

Lois Foster, Reed's wife and mother of Steve, their first born, didn't fit the mold. She typed theses for PhD candidates and did editing for John Kenneth Galbraith's book *The Liberal Hour*. And when she had time, she hung out at Harvard's School of Education. There, she encountered the early stirrings that kids in science classes learned more and better when they actually *did* things rather than read about them or listen to teachers talk.

SCENE TWO. Twenty-seven years later, Fall of 1986, Harvard Business School, 25th reunion of the class of 1961. Our class turns out in a big way for the reunion and the Business School puts on quite a show. Huge, circus-size tents dot the campus, and we are wined and dined, but with a purpose. A good three months prior to the reunion, we received a letter from our alumni class agent, urging us to make contributions to our business alma mater. The appeal is restrained and dignified, but clearly aimed at tapping into our pocketbooks and competitive instincts. The expected size of our gift is not made explicit, but its range becomes clear when we are exhorted to exceed the monetary record of the class of 1960, or better yet, the class that has the all-time record. We're talking millions of dollars from each class.

At our 25th, you didn't have to be a cryptographer to read who had "made it" in the intervening years. All you had to do was look at the names of your classmates listed on the alumni invitation. You didn't achieve that place of honor on the letterhead without giving a healthy chunk. If you still couldn't get it, the alumni association published a slick bulletin every year recognizing all contributions categorized by the amount of giving. The million-dollar-plus club was not a null set.

In a separate mailing, there was another invitation. This time from Reed Foster via our section representative, inviting us to purchase a case or two of an estate-blended Zinfandel from a boutique winery that Reed had started a few years earlier as an avocational activity.

The reunion's atmosphere was of good cheer, but the hale, hardy surface didn't have to be scratched too deeply to find painful sores of guilt. Vice presidencies in the 'big time' had been traded for broken marriages and families. Reed and Lois arrived with their promised cases of Californian Zinfandel, Reed in sandals and a multi-pocketed trout-fisherman's vest, stuffed with thumb-smudged cards and notes. He wanted to know how we liked the wine. It was oaky and deep, capturing the attention of even those of us who swigged $9.99 closeouts from the local liquor store.

SCENE THREE. August 1991. Sonoma, California. Sprawling live oaks with dangling, wispy moss, shade a boisterous party on a plateau in the hills just north of town. The smell of barbecue from grates over half-cut oil drums mixes with the pervasive smell of eucalyptus. The laughter and hearty eating mixes with clinks of empty and then full wine bottles.

This is Reed Foster at his 11th annual volunteer wine bottling, picnic and barbecue. The itinerant bottling machinery on a flatbed truck has been reserved for the weekend. The assembled family of all ages, extended family of distant cousins, a boy scout troop, and miscellaneous friends of all of the above provide the barefoot grape-smashing labor in exchange for camaraderie and good food.

In 1991, Reed is Senior Financial Partner, and joint Managing Partner in a grass roots wine-making business, hanging on by a shoe string. They had to start small, because as Reed stated, "We had no land, no grapes, and no building." It was a passion for both partners. Despite the fact that they hadn't turned a profit since their founding in 1979 and had completely depreciated years ago what few assets they owned, theirs was a mission—to create great wine, let the wine speak for itself, and market it without advertising and without snob appeal.

Their call to arms, their competitor, was not the product of other wineries, large or small, but the elitism which had enveloped the wine industry ever since a Charles de Gaulle-like French sommelier dictated that an '82 Lafite-Rothchild was unequivocally superior to an '83. With that and the highbrow rituals which had settled over the wine industry, our taste buds were no longer our own. It wasn't good enough to know what we were tasting and how we liked it. We needed some elite authority to tell us what was good and what was bad.

Reed, working in commercial real estate since graduation from the Harvard Business School, had had a life-long, absorbing interest in wine, the variations and the differentiations which gave each a distinctive personality. He was co-founder of San Francisco's wine tasting club known as the Vintner's Club. Since the club's inception in late 1973, as a ritual, they would blind taste 12 wines each Thursday afternoon. It was there he met his wine-making partner who had a golden palate. The former research chemist would, on occasion, identify the year and producer of all 12 samples. Their partnership was sealed in 1976 on a backpacking trip with Reed's son's scout troop, in the High Sierra. Reed's partner would work full-time, and Reed would do or help with the administrative functions as a sideline. Reed would not draw a salary from the winery for 12 years.

Passion trumped profits. The two built their business on the sanctity of relationships with growers, employees, distributors, and consumers. Rather than trying to outwit the other, each party to the relationship would recognize and affirm the value of what the other provided and pledged continuity to the partnership. Twenty-two vineyards in the Sonoma and Napa Valleys, screened by his partner's exacting palate and connected to the winery by Reed's financial management, dedicated their harvest to the winery. Their fermented product was distinguished by the vineyard's name and year of fermentation on the label.

Winery employees were recognized by the unique skills they brought to the community rather than their titles or positions. For example, Reed explained that their production manager angled the new wine fermentation tanks so that they could be cleaned more easily. Simple but relatively, if not completely, unique.

SCENE FOUR. It's still August, 1991. Equally passionate, Lois Foster has created The Archway School in Oakland, California. A small 90-student, K-8 independent school, it served a wide range of economic and academic backgrounds in the community, and was an entrepreneurial product of Lois' frustration with many of the city's public schools. Housed in three heavily mortgaged, made-over private residences and a former church and rectory, the United Nations teaching staff were committed to nourishing and enlivening the spirit of curiosity emanating from every kindergartener.

Lois and her staff of 16 believed most schools, public ones in particular, are extraordinarily successful in draining from their young their God-given birthright – a passion for learning. Lois was distressed by this loss of potential. It turned out she was not alone in trying to rectify this. The school had no difficulty attracting like-minded teachers, parents and students.

The school offered "at-cost" tuition, subsidized in the early years by Reed's and his father's largesse. Reed purchased the buildings over a period of time and paid the monthly mortgage when the school ran a budget in red, which it did for many years.

SCENE FIVE. It's August, 1996. Yamazaki, Japan. The wine laboratory of Suntory Limited, one of the largest purveyors of wine in Japan, is stark and clean. Electronic apparati passes out a monotonous buzz, spitting out data graphs generated by windshield-wiper pins on checkerboard square graphpaper. Interspersed are lab tables with bubbly beakers, fired by electronically controlled Bunsen burners, reminiscent of high school chemistry labs. Only this is an updated, technological extension.

This is serious business. With quiet certitude, Yutaka Zenbayashi, dressed in a stark, white lab coat, pours a $500,

1982 Chateau Lafite-Rothchild, into beakers and spiraling pipes. The French nectar courses through Dr. Zenbayashi's apparatus. It will be boiled down to a residue and analyzed for chemical makeup in gas chromatographs and spectrophotometers.

"Here, look," he announces to his assistant. "A good Bordeaux has much higher levels of pheno and amino acids, and most importantly, a subtle balance in it that achieves an intricate, full-bodied taste."

Dr. Zenbayashi, on behalf of Suntory, is using the most updated business techniques. In this case, "multi-variant analysis," to reverse engineer the production of great wines. Suntory will analyze the chemical traces of the 1982 Bordeaux, in order to recreate it for the Japanese and potentially the global market. They will use their analysis to standardize the fermentation process and calculate the exact needs of the grape cultivation. For example, they have calculated that if grape vines are pruned to an average of 2.5 leaves per bunch, optimal photosynthesis is achieved. These are familiar business school techniques, time-tested by practically every global corporation. Will they work for wine?

SCENE SIX. September, 2001. 40th year reunion, Harvard Business School, Class of 1961. Friday night, opening reception at Café Maison Robert at Boston's Old City Hall. It's a balmy, fall evening with not a hint of the impending winter. Couples and widows arrive at 6:00, in business attire, suitable for the four course dinner at 8:00. We spill out into the open courtyard with our complimentary glasses of Zinfandel and Chardonnay.

Reed has not let us down in either libations nor costume. The trout vest has all the appearances of a 15 year veteran. Reed, with a slightly whiter beard, doesn't appear to be any the worse for the 15 years since the last reunion. Close observers might have detected, however an extra twinkle in his eye. Even on the first day of class in September in 1959, it was clear Reed wasn't one to telegraph his thoughts or feelings. Nevertheless, his smile that evening seemed bolder and more attenuated. He could've been carrying a secret that he was dying to tell and even boast about, but the cumulative years of personality wouldn't allow its release. Then, too, the exchange of pleasantries of the assembled would periodically stop as a whispered piece of gossip spread around the courtyard. Between the salad course and entrée and the obligatory thank you's to the classmates who had organized the reunion, our section's secretary proposed a toast and the rabbit came jumping out of the hat.

A month earlier, Reed Foster's Ravenswood winery had been sold to Constellation Brands. Reed's share: $12 million, all cash. There was no way that Reed would ever say it, let alone think it, but it was clear to me that what was missing was a thundering bellow, "How's that, big boys?"

EPILOGUE 1: Just Before the Credits

It turned out that Reed's and Lois' first act after receiving his check from Constellation Brands was to consolidate the mortgages on Archway School's four buildings, now profitable and financially stable, and donate them to the school.

EPILOGUE 2:

The Suntory winery has won Japan's coveted Demming Award for quality control but its wines aren't winning any prizes. After analyzing 62 wines from France, California, and Australia, Suntory began producing Thomi, a $100 bottle of Cabernet Sauvignon, Cabernet Franc, and Merlot Grapes, that is named after a local hill. Suntory's catalogue calls it a "masterpiece of masterpieces, the fruit of our technology." During a blind taste test of 6 wines that Suntory arranged, the Sommelier at Tokyo's Takanawa Prince Hotel declared 5 of the mystery wines "excellent"; they proved to be French. One other he deemed "a total flop"; it was Suntory's Thomi. "It has an intolerable bouquet of dirt and is thin and flat." He added, "Anybody that sells that stuff with pride is deceiving himself."

How exceptional that my dear HBS co-conspirator, Reed, did, in fact, create a wine to be proud of.

SEEKING FULLNESS

It's MAY 13, 2005, CLOSING in on 9:00 pm, the final hour of my last class of a 40-year career as a professor in graduate schools of management at Harvard, Stanford, and Tulane, and a 30-year tenure at Boston University. As mentioned previously, the majority of that time, I taught organizational behavior and leadership with the latter assuming a larger portion of my energies in the last twenty years. I ended up teaching leadership, if you believe in fate, as a result of my family name. But most assuredly, my aspiration had been to help create responsible and imaginative corporate and nonprofit leaders.

The twenty-five MBA students in the classroom are restless and so am I. We both want closure and it comes from an unexpected source. A bagpiper marches into the classroom, followed by family members Kristin, Jody, Wren, and Paul. Lucy is holding a large frosted sheet cake topped with several brown, miniature, plastic horses. A white stallion has escaped the diminutive plastic fence and stands high on its haunches in a Hi-Oh Silver mimic.

As Lucy cuts and distributes the cake, I'm shaking hands and receiving both well wishes on my retirement and congratulations on an excellent class. Four students said it was the best class they had ever taken and subsequent teacher and course student-ratings confirm that this had been a particularly memorable semester-long learning experience for the students and, as a matter of fact, for me too.

I was pleased with my finale, but left with a sweet and sour aftertaste. It was sweet to hear the generous appreciation I received that night and also throughout my long teaching career, which by conservative estimates would include well over 3,000 students. I genuinely believe I left most of my students with new insights about themselves and the organizational world. Plus, I offered ways they could improve it and themselves. All of this felt good.

The sour, on the other hand, was prompted by questions which I couldn't let go of: Was there a better way of expressing my humanistic values than preparing private sector leaders in university and corporate settings? What was Lucy signaling with her carefully configured horse figures on the cake with one clearly busting out of his pen? These queries gave rise to reflecting on the messages about success that I'd come to believe from childhood and subsequent years. What did I actually feel was most important in life?

My most prized high school achievement left no such ambiguity. I fulfilled the parental directive that upgrading one's status was a priority and went out for football and a varsity-lettered jacket in my junior year. This value was particularly pushed by my mom. Essentially a country girl with a quick mind and a talent for playing piano by ear, she and my high school-graduate father mingled within a circle of professionals. They eventually ascended into a wealthy neighborhood, well beyond their Spartan, rural, and educationally-deprived upbringing. Dad's shrewd stock market investments on his meager middle-manager salary were the ticket for their social climb. While he clearly took pride in his ability to increase his net worth, this was not his exclusive priority, as his charitable work and anonymous donations to his church would later attest to.

My folks conveyed no ambiguity about my going to college. Neither of them had gone and only a handful of my high school classmates did, but the unspoken message from my parents and our friends was that a college education was a pass-go card for success. Mine, as you've read, initially led to an engineering degree, a wife, two kids, and a job with Boeing Aircraft in Seattle. Though that turned out to be a vacant aspiration. Engineering calculations were tedious, boring, and quite frankly a little beyond my natural aptitude. The missile I was assigned to design at Boeing (along with a team of engineers), would huff and puff on the launch pad, but never lift more than five feet off the ground. Unceremoniously, it would lie down on its concrete pad like a wounded dog. If Iowa State College of Engineering and Agriculture didn't fulfill its initial promise, it did provide new life options.

I had discovered leadership, but in the late 1970s and 80s, I questioned how true to my humanistic values were my daily practices. Who were the beneficiaries of my efforts? Was preparing the leaders of corporate America what I wanted to spend my time and energy doing?

My first taste of a culture different from my own resulted from an invitation to co-lead a principal development academy for the Boston Public Schools. Latino, African American, South American, Asian, and Caucasian teachers (male and female, young and old), had already proven themselves as successful urban educators and were preparing for the challenges of school leadership. Responsive and appreciative, their eyes shone with excitement as they eagerly participated in a robust, Socratic, back-and-forth case discussion. More, more, they wanted more. We hadn't finished the first session when I knew this could be a future calling.

Fast forward fifteen years and look into another classroom. This time, one in The Educator Leadership Institute, which I co-founded with Tom Scott in Waltham, Massachusetts. Again, there are principal-to-be candidates but they are finishing, rather than starting their preparation. I designed a learning-by-doing program with few lectures and many assignments requiring candidates to solve real world school administrator problems. I recruited Ilana Bedchick into my program even though she couldn't quite imagine herself as a principal. At that point, the reason for her enrollment was the prospect of becoming a more effective teacher leader. We both took a risk on her potential as a principal-leader and her initial performance in the program suggested we might lose the bet.

Early on, Ilana's mindset struggled to leave behind a classroom mentality when called to embrace a vision of the school as a whole. Once she "got it," however, with a little help from the faculty and myself who acted more as coaches than professors, Ilana was well on her way to make the transition from teacher to school leader.

I proudly watched this petite woman, with a bundle of curly hair that extended her height by a third, give her final presentation to classmates and the faculty of the Educator Leadership Institute. It was a warm-up and practice talk to a hypothetical audience of school personnel interviewing her for a principalship. Her PowerPoint presentation exhibited articulate strength and knowledge. Calm and assured, she explained what she had learned over the previous 16 months and focused on why she was the candidate of choice.

A year later, she moved west with her fiancé. With over 350 applicants for nine principalships, the overwhelming majority coming from within the system, Ilana, was chosen to lead a Seattle elementary school (after an extensive and exhausting interview process), in one of the city's most poverty-stricken areas. The Seattle Public Schools' decision confirmed her particularly strong credentials.

I'm proud of Ilana, as I am of the 100+ graduates of my 7-year-old academy. Not all of them carried Ilana's sparkle of accomplishment, but every graduate believed they could more confidently lead in public schools than when they entered. This was the program's guarantee and purpose. From her "Day 1" as an educator, Ilana practiced teacher-leadership in some of the toughest schools. She mentored new teachers immediately after earning her own professional status.

All of my program's graduates' growth as educational leaders prompted my own epiphany. The Educator Leadership Institute had given me a fullness which had previously escaped me. I had become a prime mover for over 100 educational leaders' who offered undeniable, valuable contributions in their leadership positions.

Lucy's prescient white stallion who waded through frosting three years earlier had kicked free of artificial constraints and found a new and renewing pasture.

TANGO

COME DREAM WITH ME. PUSH forward in time. It's Wednesday morning, 1:30 a.m., March 10th, 2010, in Buenos Aires, Argentina. Michael, Elaine, Lucy, and I are at the Ideal, the oldest and most well-known tango dance hall in South America. At this moment, the milonga, the Argentinean community dance, is building to its crescendo. The tango orchestra (an accordion-like bandoneon, piano, violin, and bass), broadcasts a syncopated eight-line beat, accompanying a rich baritone lead singer who croons "Por una Cabeza." (Translated, it means "By a Head" which will prove prescient.) Low chandeliers softly light a nineteenth century, ornately-carved, wooden ceiling and cast a light on the oval dance floor below.

The couples are collectively in a trance, puppets to the orchestra's haunting rhythms, gliding effortlessly in the counterclockwise line of dance around the oval floor. They follow the etiquette of: no talk, no looking at others, save for navigational purposes. They are collapsed into each other, chest to chest, cheek to cheek, with the woman's left arm sensually draped across her partner's shoulder and the man's arm possessively encompassing her waist. Temporarily invested in each other, each couple moves and spins in perfect synchronization.

In these pre-dawn moments, the couples have coalesced into a collective of one, a ritual codified by Argentinean and Uruguayan ancestry, but currently practiced the world over.

Michael and I know without speaking, a nod does it, the time has come. This will be the climax and test of our yearlong efforts.

Michael and I have been dancing interchangeably with our wives, Lucy and Elaine, but now we must invite other women to dance. It is part of the ritual. Of course, they will accept. They have seen us on the dance floor with our wives, and we look like promising dance partners. The two of us are rightly attired. Michael, 6'2", at fifty-five is a devastatingly handsome African American male with a slim dancer's build. He is clothed in a draped, but bodily-tailored, mauve, silk polo shirt, black trousers, and a neck choker of tiny beads and shells, all of which are accentuated by his black skin, glistening with perspiration. My Italian shirt with subtle vertical stripes of black, gold and brown, has its sleeves rolled part way up to the elbow to allow accentuation of my bold, Navajo-executed, turquoise-encrusted bracelet. Michael and I telegraph elegant sophistication and Buenos Aireans delight in the exotic. We are made more appealing by our matching tango shoes: black patent leather with blue suede accents. (Michael searched every shoe store in the city to find the *piéce de résistance*, and I had to have a matching pair.)

Our test this evening is not in the ladies' acceptance of our invitation of a first dance, but our reputation in being an acceptable partner for subsequent engagements. Word travels fast at a milonga. If we are not up to the standard, we risk losing out in dancing with the most well-dressed and accomplished women. Their eyes will be diverted when we look their way, or they might demure, saying they have previously accepted the invitation of another. We would miss the real adrenaline producing excitement of a community milonga where the exchange of partners is essential to the enjoyment and the opportunity to have, albeit fleetingly, a close physical relationship with another. In my dream, Michael and I, in full partnership and close participation with our wives, have made the sacrifices to prepare for this ultimate test of whether or not we have fully stitched Argentinean tango into our being. Can this dream come true? Will it happen?

Change the time focus. The dream and Olympian training to prepare for it started in March, 2009, when the four of us challenged our Boston-based tango class skills by flying to Buenos Aires. For two weeks, we immersed ourselves 24/7 both in tango classes, taught by demanding but colorful masters, and their sultry, sensually-clad assistants, and by attending early morning milongas. Imagine consuming four perspiring classes a day washed down with an Argentinean cabernet of a milonga from 11 pm to 3 am in the morning. Buenos Aires outdoes Paris as a beautiful, vibrant, fun-loving city, plus it is hospitable and generous to a fault.

All four of us were deeply affected by our two weeks in the spring of 2009, but Michael and I were spiritually moved. Our souls are given life by dancing; we must dance as a fulfillment of who we are. Tango became the ultimate expression of ourselves after a lifetime consumed by other dances.

Michael interrupted his medical education to spend two years as a professional dancer in New York City. For the last eight years (while pursuing a highly distinguished career as a medical clinician, researcher, and the first African American tenured full professor at the Harvard Medical School), he's given himself over to a variety of community dance performances, including starring as Drosselmeyer in the Urban Nutcracker. Known as the "Dancing Doctor," he continued to dance in Boston-area productions of the Black Nativity for years.

It's not happenstance. Both of us met our wives dancing. Elaine and Michael were in the same dance company. Lucy and I met on the dance floor of a holiday party. And, if truth be known, my first wife Joan and I met at a dance mixer on the first day of college. Dancing is part of my DNA, and the chromosomes have spun out into my family, even those unrelated by blood. When dancing, Michael and I are deliciously vulnerable. Nothing is hidden. We are out there, ready to give and receive.

Prior to our March, 2009, holiday in Buenos Aires, Michael and I had a casual relationship. We were active members of First Parish in Brookline, and our sons sang in the same acapella boys' choir. But our time together in Buenos Aires galvanized my dream of us proving ourselves at the Ideal dance hall. We would be two guys from the States, a dance pro and an amateur, bonded together by following the path of actor Robert Duvall to become masters of Argentinean tango. It would be a realization of life quests, the outcome of life trajectories which had pre-ordained our coming to Buenos Aires.

In my dream, from March 2009 to 2010, the four of us worked hard. Damn, we worked. Tango lessons plus practice milongas twice weekly. You don't just learn Argentinean tango footsteps. You assimilate a way of being with your partner. Both must know and practice the language of the dance, but the rapport between the partners separates the prosaic from the mystical. Yes, the male leads, but only with the concurrence of the female. A subtle reciprocity ensues, so delicate that the two become one.

SWINGS BETWEEN
HUMANISM AND SPIRITUALITY

I BELIEVE IN THE INHERENT WORTH and dignity of every person. Reflecting on my life trajectory, albeit a rocky liftoff and frequently wayward course, I recognize I have been guided by a mission to actualize this belief by coaching and teaching others to reach their full intellectual and emotional potential, particularly those who aspire to be leaders. To actualize this vision, I have found it essential to build supportive communities of practice, as well as to open heart and mind to the relationships which nourish me.

My dad bequeathed to me a spirit of generosity and concern for others. At his funeral, the pastor of the large, affluent, suburban, Presbyterian church revealed that my parents had, years earlier, anonymously given a large endowment, which begged recognition at my father's memorial. Two images of Dad are my reminders of his heritage. One: Dad, upon his retirement, is driving his newly washed, powder-beige Cadillac, the car of his dreams and symbol of his worldly accomplishments, to deliver daily "meals on wheels" to the infirm and housebound of the less fortunate. He did this daily, for a number of years, all the while sitting on a several million-dollar estate.

I keep the second reminder framed in my office. On the masthead of the *Boston Globe*, May 28, 1982 (the day of Lucy and my marriage), he wrote a "bit of advice." Mom was traditionally, I should say always, the spokesperson of the two, but this time she compelled Dad to compose and deliver their blessing at our minister- and rabbi-less backyard ceremony. That morning, Mom went shopping at Bloomingdale's, and Dad sat in his Cadillac reading the *Globe* and penning the words to be delivered later at our marriage ceremony, which are as follows: "Each of you say to the other 'I love you' frequently. It is a theme you will love to hear and it will be the cement which will keep you happy and together." I can confirm Dad's wisdom.

Mom was a moral authority, which had been both a blessing and a challenge. For her, there was always a right and wrong, and she did not hesitate to speak out on these standards. Sorting out what is truly right and wrong for myself has been a lifelong quest, a journey for which I hold Mom appreciatively responsible. During my growing up, very little room between black and white existed in her moral code or my own. I was an unquestioning and unwitting believer. A prisoner of her moral code so much so, it precipitated a break up with my high school freshman-year girlfriend, Mary, because she was Roman Catholic. Picture Mary and I walking hand in hand down Big Ben Boulevard, the main thoroughfare of our community. Mother slowly drives by, eyes welded on Mary. Terrorized, Mary dives into the bushes because I had told her the disdain my mother held for her. I stand paralyzed, denying Mary's dignity and my integrity. This still reverberates as a painful lesson I won't forget.

Maplewood-Richmond Heights Senior High was a venue for another life lesson, this time of a more positive character. The scene: my deliverance from wimp to super boy, at least in my own eyes. At this wrong-side-of-the-tracks school, athletic prowess reigned supreme. Class nerds were frequently ridiculed, and only a few of us went on to a university. As a male, you were nothing unless you wore a varsity letter jacket. In my junior year, I woke up to the fact that I was rapidly approaching zero status because I hadn't participated in any sports. Blackening my peculiarly soft hands with zinc oxide to prevent excessive bleeding, I went out for varsity football. It was hell. Only Kirk Swann and I had failed to go out for freshman or Junior Varsity football, but I made the team and notched not only a varsity letter, but also a giant uplift in self-confidence and my capacity to take hold of my life.

Next came Iowa State College of Engineering and Agriculture (in the middle of a statewide, long cornfield), which offered an opportunity to practice those newfound leadership skills gained at Camp Miniwanca. Only a mediocre engineering student, and certainly no athlete, I plunged into student activities, fraternity politics, ROTC, and the Presbyterian church, to differentiate myself from those less talented, organized, and pious. This was all in the service of demonstrating that I was a leader other than by name alone. I was president of this, vice-president of that, commander of the ROTC unit, with 500 cadets saluting me weekly. Sunday morning found me in the pulpit reading slickly worded prayers lifted from a book of prayers written by the Chaplain of the United States Senate. Looking back, I can't say I was a fraud or duplicitous, but a lot of my leadership was for show, with only skin-deep soulfulness. I applied to McCormick Theological Seminary on the basis of a delusional Elmore Gantry vision of myself in a scarlet robe, arms uplifted, exhorting the word to a worshipful congregation.

As Lieutenant Gerald C. Leader, Company Commander, A Company, 4th Battalion, 23rd Infantry Training Regiment, stationed at Fort Leonard Wood, Missouri, I was no longer in the same cultural and political bubble I had occupied the previous 23 years. *Leave it to Beaver* was nowhere in sight.

The good, hardworking, God-fearing, churchgoing people had evaporated. Commissioned only three months earlier, I was thrust into a command position usually occupied by captain-ranked officers with at least 10 years' experience. The Pentagon was clean out of captains, so greenhorn Lt. Leader was given 220 recruits to train, and to assist me, 30 non-commissioned officers, 25 who were Black (the first persons of color I'd ever talked to).

There was no room for artifice; no superficial Christianity; no playing at leadership. This was hard-edge, brutally real, and unforgiving. I wasn't in a war zone, but it had characteristics of one. I was responsible for recruits' daily lives. My days were spent teaching my charges not to get killed by live ammunition. Recruits were not my only problem. One of the Platoon Sergeants in the regiment was caught pimping his daughter to my recruits. I presided over multiple shotgun marriages in my office between pregnant brides-to-be (hustled there by anxious mothers), and new recruits who had used their last night in town to sack their sweethearts. The word-heavy and practice-light Christianity I brought to the fort wasn't up to this reality test.

Disillusioned, it became clear my next stop would not be a seminary, but instead the Harvard Business School, the citadel of capitalism and fierce competition, which played, at least on the surface, with an established good ol' boys' etiquette. Ironically, it was there that I found an outlet for my humanistic predispositions. A relatively new discipline pioneered by the Business School, called human relations, captured my imagination and sense of purpose. For me, and many other latent humanists, the field, later to be labeled 'organizational behavior,' was something more than an academic social science discipline, the study of people in organizations. It was a calling to transform America's workplace into a more democratically run and participative community that actualized the highest potential of every employee, supervisor, and executive. We were going to neutralize the effects of top-down corporate hierarchies and release the long-stifled creativity of every working American. And we, as future faculty members, were going to prepare our students with tools to do the same.

When I graduated in 1965 with an MBA and Doctorate, I had a spiritual mission and credentials to practice it. Teaching organizational behavior and leadership to graduate business students at Stanford, Harvard, Tulane, and Boston Universities was a 40-year career preoccupation that satisfied my need to be societally purposeful and allowed me to leverage my academic status and apparent knowledge for a small management consulting and executive development practice, which supplemented my somewhat spare academic salary.

Through teaching and consulting, I believe I had a small humanizing effect on my students, as well as American and several global corporations. I am proud of this. At Boston University, as Department Chairman for seven years, I utilized a talent that served me well in the past and continues to do so: recruiting high quality talent with values similar to my own. Four of my hires in the late 1970s and early 80s, all of whom are humanists in the best sense, still teach at the school, despite an enormous turnover of other faculty in the last 25 years. This is a legacy I keep dear in my heart.

In the late 1980s, I proposed to the School of Management faculty a new elective course called "Leadership." They denied the request, arguing that leadership couldn't be taught: you were either born with it or not. I reapplied and relabeled the course "The Art of Management," which was accepted, and taught it using all the previously gathered materials. Rightfully renamed "Leadership" several years later, it has been an ever-popular cornerstone of the curriculum, taught every semester by at least four other faculty. The guiding philosophy of the course is that true leadership comes from within: soulful expression of an individual's talents and capacities.

Troubling, in retrospect, was how much I was influenced as a faculty member of the Schools of Business and Management by its dictates and the opportunism of client consulting issues. The message of my course in consulting represented what I consider the humanistic "right thing to do," but while based upon a humanistic philosophy, it might have been more pointed in the critique of issues I faced. Advancing corporate and shareholder value frequently took priority over employee integrity and rights. Now it is clear, that the world-changing, headlong idealist of my 30s and 40s became compromised by the hard realities of earning a living and making my way in the academic world.

However, starting in the early 1990s and extending to the present, I shifted my professional efforts to preparing public school leaders. Usually, the candidates are teachers who aspire to be public school principals. My first taste of training another population of candidates came when I was invited to co-lead a principal development academy for the Boston Public Schools. The students' leadership skills were limited, but they were eager, responsive, and appreciative. We hadn't finished the first session when I knew this would be my future calling. Preparing MBAs and corporate executives to optimize our capitalist system had held my attention for over 30 years, but by the end of the 20th century, any improvements appeared to be only incremental. Corporate social responsibility and the leverage achieved in corporate productivity from involvement of employees in decision-making are now well-established.

Public school leadership, in contrast, remains largely undeveloped, though this is no particular fault of the individuals involved. They haven't been trained. The licensing requirements for public school principals up to the late 1990s were a joke. A teacher's license and a couple of dreary classroom courses were all that was required, yet demands for high student and school performance, occasioned by NCLB legislation and the high-stakes MCAS test, increased the complexity of the principal's job a hundred-fold.

In 2002, I founded and continued to run until 2012, a principal preparation academy, The Educator Leadership Institute (ELLI). It took in approximately 25 candidates a year and subsequently graduated them with a Massachusetts Department of Education Administrative license and Master's Degree, credentials this institute was authorized to give. I'm proud of our graduates and exhilarated that I've had a hand in their development and accomplishments. Many graduates have progressed to significant leadership roles. My professional work shifted into alignment with my core values: assisting others to actualize their human potential, particularly those who aspire to be leaders. Preparing educational leaders, who in turn guide the learning and development of others, gives me particular pleasure and a sense of fulfillment.

Of course, another major life arena expands our hearts and minds, grows our spiritual and humanistic tendencies: relationships. Fortunately, starting in the 1960s, my daughters Jody and Kristie (and later their partners), my life partner Lucy and our son Wren, and our three grandchildren, Michela, Jerilyn, and Emily, would have a profound effect on my deepening spiritual development. With much regret, I admit it took a while to let them into my world and me into theirs. Jody and Kristie were born in 1961 and 1963 respectively, calling forth both the joys of fatherhood and its inherent responsibilities. However, the latter carried a greater weight than finding unalloyed delight in these precious beings. Will I finish my dissertation, will I find a job, will I be tenured, were professional preoccupations further exacerbated by an ambivalence whether to repair or quit a failing marriage.

Once my first marriage had ended, I found myself in New Orleans while my daughters lived with their mother in Lexington, Massachusetts. I allowed myself to acknowledge the emotional attachment I felt for them, heightened by the separation. Back-and-forth visits and a summer together intensified my desire to return to Boston. In 1974, Boston University accommodated me. All the joy and love I have experienced with them, their husbands, and family is incalculable. Their progeny, along with Wren's, are a never-ending source of devotion, pride, and renewal. They keep reminding me of growth possibilities when the odds look bleak. I feel so fortunate that our families lived three blocks from one another.

Likewise, I have come to believe that Lucy and I finding each other as life partners is best expressed by a term from her heritage, the Yiddish "*beshert*," meaning destined or meant-to-be. Both of us having left first marriages (but more mature for the experience), were drawn to each other by shared values, deep appreciation of the arts, a need for spiritual observance, and finally and most significantly - a mutual love. Her generosity of spirit, concern for others, and positive outlook has had a deep and lasting influence on my life, from which I see myself a more spiritual person.

The last five years or so have been particularly fulfilling and joyful for me. I believe I am living a life closer than ever before with my humanistic aspirations, and I hold Lucy and my relationship with her in large measure responsible. She loves and believes in me and my capacities, which frequently exceeds my own: a standard which challenges me to live at my best. I regretfully admit it is only recently that I've been able to internalize her disarmingly powerful message.

As Wren was born in 1985, I was able to be more present to the joys and pains of fatherhood. Vivid is the memory of racing around with him wailing his head off in a bassinet and me trying to find an exit door in the large auditorium where I was giving an exam to over 200 students, only to trip an emergency exit alarm, which magnified the pandemonium. Students received five bonus points on their final exams for "extraordinary circumstances." By the end of the 20th century, I thought I had crafted a damn good life for my family and myself and smugly believed I was the prime mover in this creation. I was restlessly content, the oxymoron intended and descriptive.

Then came 9/11, which jolted my consciousness and subconsciousness in ways I am only now becoming aware. Let me tell you the story, but before I do, I have to mention the state of my theological questioning before 9/11.

Steven Weinberg's little catch phase kept chasing me: "The more the universe seems comprehensible, the more it also seems pointless." The more comprehensible, the more pointless; that's big and abstract, but its mind-gnawing. I couldn't seem to let go of it. Steven Weinberg, a Nobel prize-winning physicist, placed the phrase at the end of his 1977 best-selling book, *The First Three Minutes*. When I read it, it jangled me and kept fermenting. Then came 9/11.

That day, I'm in the School of Management building where I teach and have my office. For better or worse, we have a Starbucks in the building, and I'm standing in a long line, annoyed at myself that I hadn't timed my arrival to avoid the morning migration of undergraduate business majors for their daily fix of caffeine. CNN, piped in on an overhead screen, is holding our attention, as we wait in line. It's not unusual for us to gawk in unison, and we stare at what seems to be a fire in one of the towers of the World Trade Center. I remember how yesterday there was a storage tank fire in Chelsea, but the smoke was much darker. The monitor's too far away to read the running script, and the line is trying my patience. I'm fidgety and go back to my office.

By 9 o'clock, I feel a headache coming on. There is no student jabber, just sullen looks in the elevator ride down from the 6th to the 2nd floor, back to Starbucks. It's a surreal scene of over 100 silent, frozen gawkers watching Armageddon on TV monitors. Maybe this is a movie. No, it couldn't be. There is the incessant chirping "Chai soy latte…double espresso grande."

A glance at the screen sends me reeling to a chair. Both towers have collapsed, leaving two smoldering, eviscerated stumps. I gasp for breath and momentarily faint, my head on a table on crossed arms.

"Are you OK?" someone asks.

"Yeah, yeah, I'm fine" I reply. But I'm really not.

"Let me get you some water."

"OK."

After a few minutes, I raise my head, take a sip, and look at the monitor. The image of the two beheaded, leveled towers won't go away. I lay my head down, my body is on fire, mind racing, desperately trying to avoid a forbidden memory. But no use, I'm carried back, back in time over forty years earlier to 1958, to Fort Leonard Wood, Missouri.

I am transformed back into the basic training company commander I was at Fort Leonard Wood, mentioned earlier, an army post that seemed to cling to the inhospitable, scorched red clay. That hot July morning, I took my 220 acne-faced, flat-topped, gawky kids to the hand grenade throwing range which was a checkerboard of seven-foot-high concrete bunkers.

Pentagon policy required every soldier to throw two live grenades in order to qualify as an infantryman.

Managing a pose of calm and assurance, I explained the exercise: pull the grenade pin, count to 10, then throw the live grenade over a ten-foot-high concrete bunker wall. I led the practice with dummy grenades before issuing live ones in the afternoon. With heart pounding, in a cold sweat, I demonstrated with a live grenade, the wide sweep of the arm before the deliberate release.

"Fire in the hole!" I shouted before the explosion on the other side of the concrete wall.

I surveyed my recruits and non-commissioned officers. Sergeant Campbell, a ten-year army veteran, had seen combat in Korea. You felt at ease in his presence. He understood why I assigned him to be Bill's coach through the day's exercises. It was suspect why Bill had been allowed to be in the company. He had been seriously coordination-challenged.

"Bill, keep your goddamn head down," I barked.

I was just about ready to start the grenade-throwing exercise when a premature, violent explosion rattled my head. I, Second Lieutenant Leader, twenty-three-year-old Company Commander, ran to the site of the explosion at the training awrea, pushing away others in my path. I stood traumatized, gasping for breath. The putrid smell of burned blood and the sight before me convulsed my stomach. I needed to throw up, but command etiquette wouldn't allow it. Before me were two eviscerated bodies. My mind, blanked by an excruciating headache demanded: "Damn, do something!" But it was too late.

Although the Army Staff Judge Advocate inquiry following the tragedy found no error or fault on the part of the grenade range staff, those in my command, or me, I still feel complicit in those two soldiers' deaths. The inquiry did find that the physician examining Bill for his entrance to the Army noted for the record that it looked as if his motor skills were mildly compromised, but not even close to the standard to reject him. One theory held, that Bill's grip froze on the grenade after pulling the pin and he could not release it. The positioning of Bill's and Campbell's bodies suggested Campbell had vainly attempted to wrestle the grenade from Bill's grasp.

The Universe seemed quite incomprehensible those days. They and their violent deaths will always be with me: as living persons and as the image of two dead bodies. After that day, I could not keep a training command; the constant exposure to violence was too much. I requested and was reassigned to be the Post Public Information Officer. For 57 years, I have never fired a weapon and studiously avoid violent movies and TV shows.

After 9/11, perhaps needing balm for our souls, Lucy, Wren, and I made a pilgrimage to Chartres in France. Once there, I knew it had been predetermined. The hour train ride from Paris through sumptuous farmland, even in winter, built an uneasy anticipation.

We stepped out of the station and Wren asked, "Should we get a taxi?"

No need. To our immediate left, dominating the skyline, were a different set of twin towers. One was a smooth cone, and the second, seeming like its half-brother not spoken to in years, was an elaborate and pretentious Romanesque wedding cake. It appeared more concerned with its attractiveness than any spiritual purpose.

For an hour and a half, we became part of the flock shepherded through Chartres by Malcom Miller, a guide of 44 years. It was his life's mission, and he had Chartres talk to us, no, touch us; I would not be the same afterwards. At first, he was an English don from BBC central casting, with unkempt white hair, a disarmingly attractive British accent, and a dollop of dry wit, making his living as a tour guide. But quickly he became context for the Biblical characters of the stained-glass windows, which told us their stories.

The stained-glass window hung on the south wall of the cathedral, and even on that dull day, was luminous. The 12th century medieval message was unmistakably and powerfully executed and trivialized modern-day movie animation. Malcom Miller read the story of the window, allowing me the luxury of total visual and textural absorption. I'm familiar with the Adam and Eve story, but his narrative, told in a Charlton Heston God-like voice, took me on an unexpected therapeutic journey.

Starting at the lower left, moving right, God creates Adam. God, stern-faced, is identified by a brilliant red halo, and uses a green tube to blow life into a naked, hairless Adam, who looks like he has just been hatched.

In the second pane, Miller instructs: "Adam likes God's garden, but feels vulnerable and lonely. His hand reaches out and nervously grips a succulent bush."

Oh God, I knew this story. It was a cliché, but I couldn't get enough of the stained-glass kaleidoscope. Out from Adam's rib, a fiercely determined God yanks Eve. The two naked first beings on Earth are clearly lonely, and I'm feeling their anxiety. I'm there with them.

Temptation to eat the forbidden fruit from the Tree of Knowledge of Good and Evil comes next. The medieval mythmaker punctuates Eve's seduction with a coiling, red serpent, who in turn double-dares Adam to take a bite of the shimmering red apple. "Oh, come on, big boy, just a little taste." Of course he does, and thankfully. Where would we be if he refused?

Adam chokes, grabs his Adam's apple, but it's too late. All hell breaks loose, and I, as a Homosapien, will never be the same. The second to last stained-glass pane, foretells the release of satanic forces, which will forever be with us. And we must laboriously make our own goodness; we decide.

The next window's biblical story evinces deep philosophical querying within me. Also, honestly, I'm horrified. Cain (first born in the human race), in a brilliant yellow waist coast, against a cobalt blue background, has just lodged an arm's-length hoe into his brother Abel's brain. From Cain's demonized face and posture, it's clear that this was not the result of a fit of anger. It was a deliberate and calculated murder. Cain has pushed Abel to the ground with his left foot, and the arc of the deadly blow is unmistakably clear from how deep the axe has penetrated his brother's skull. At the second before impact, Abel turns and looks at Cain quizzically.

I'm repulsed. Humankind's second decision is a violent act that couldn't have been more ghastly, but ironically, it's also relieving. Violence has been with us from the beginning. It is I who have allowed the specter of violence to shadow me. I walked away with two options: treat the world as pointless, with random causation, or revitalize my efforts to create a more humanistic destiny.

When I review my life for potent influences related to the person I have evolved into being, my mentor for over 13 years, Jay O'Callahan, comes to mind. His stories and storytelling extol the wonderment of life. An awe-inspiring model, Jay's subtle guidance and repeated affirmations for my stories have been the wellspring for delivering any gifts I might have for witnessing and writing narrative. He opened creative windows in me that I didn't know existed.

Having heard several of Jay's High Street stories on cassette tape, I was primed to meet the golden-tongued author in 1997 at a weekend workshop he gave on "Creativity Through Storytelling." I wasn't disappointed. The group was diverse in age, gender, and occupation, and we couldn't let go of Jay, or each other, on the Sunday evening of our departure. Hence, our writing retreats with him over the last thirty years. With Jay's prompts and participation, we write and tell stories, perform improvisational theater, and create mini-operas out of our collective subconscious and questionable musical talents. It's legitimized adult play at its best.

Early on, Jay gave us a precious gift: we didn't need others' criticism or suggestions. Appreciation of how we were touched by a story or performance respected the integrity of the creator and primed a continuous bubbling of imagination. After each creation, Jay calls for performance "appreciations," never critiques. Thus, he has trained us to be keen observers, if not connoisseurs, of tactile, auditory, visual, visceral, and verbal subtleties.

Jay's mentorship spawned the "Creative Monsters," as we call ourselves. All of us, including Jay, have been beneficiaries of this life-giving and life-affirming community. Our times together are a spiritual experience comparable to my participation in First Parish.

Two years of my life, from 2005 to 2007, awakened a spirituality I had not previously experienced. The trauma of potentially losing my grandchild, Jerilyn, to Aplastic Anemia and then witnessing the life-giving miracle of their bone-marrow transplant, deepened my spiritual awareness and generated a renewed gratitude for their life and life as a whole. Joining and participating in First Parish's community confirmed that I needn't be alone in my pain, spiritual longings, and journey. I have found others, such as Reverend Martha, who shared my quest and provided comforting and challenging guidance. I am grateful that my entire life has been enriched with humanism and spirituality.

FAMILY

COLORS

The soft, dusty pink deepening to a
Chinese orange-red waits for
expression until he knows we will
appreciate his special glory.

Mischievously I have tried to secretly
spy on him and witness his color
show when no one is around; but no, he
is clever and keeps his cheeks pale white
until an audience arrives. Then
and only then, Asher's cheeks explode
with a technicolor smile. It's
transformative.

Conrad Leader

My adolescent summers were spent listening, enthralled, to the stories of my paternal grandfather, Conrad, telling how he crafted a life. I'll share with you several I found particularly memorable.

Born in 1880, Conrad grew up on a farm in the German-speaking region of Switzerland with nine siblings and an authoritarian, religious zealot father who commanded he prepare for the Catholic priesthood as his life's occupation. This seemed particularly ludicrous since Conrad (from early childhood), had displayed a rebellious predisposition. He had secretly loaded the town's ceremonial cannon with rocks and on feast day early one morning, he ignited the cannon and leveled the church's shed that housed the church's milk cow, which fortunately was not in attendance.

Publicly thrashed and quarantined to solitary confinement for a month by his tyrannical father, Conrad was ready to escape. Anticipating the need for craft to support himself when he was on his own, he secretly apprenticed himself to an older brother who had learned butchering skills.

With his recently acquired knowledge, Conrad fled to Paris which temporarily provided employment at a market until French authorities disallowed German hands of massaging their decidedly French lamb chops.

What to do? Where to go? Newly made friends in Paris advised him to travel to St. Louis, Missouri, USA, where a world's fair had just opened in 1904. There had to be a German-speaking Swiss exhibit needing butchering.

Passage to the States was on a barely seaworthy steamer, but at the right price. The passenger manifest at Ellis Island records a Conrad Ledergerber entering the port with forty U.S. dollars in his pocket and leaving with an iconic American surname, Leader.

St. Louis proved to be everything Conrad could have hoped for: A job at the 1904 World's Fair and after its closing, employment at a German-speaking butchery. Seiler's Meat Market was more than an occupational find. Edna, Seiler's strikingly beautiful 14-year-old, eldest daughter and Conrad fell in love with each other. The age differential, a little over ten years, made any thought of marriage inconceivable by Edna's parents.

All was not lost, however. Conrad, again demonstrating exceptional problem-solving capacity, proposed a prenuptial agreement where he would move to Idaho in hopes to prosper and return to St. Louis to marry Edna, which he did. They did, in fact, move to Idaho to start their life together, but under the conditions that they would return to Missouri after twenty-five years to be close to Edna's family.

Conrad and Edna, along with three other families, founded the town of Downey, Idaho. Of course, Leader's Meat Market was at its center. This proved to be a comfortable yet insecure arrangement for Conrad, Edna and their son John Conrad, my father. With the constant threat of disabling droughts, each year brought the worry of having sufficient water for human, livestock and agricultural needs.

Conrad's life story, as noted already, was one of not letting major negative forces impact him without attempting some remedial response.

As I listened to Conrad over time, I heard a person who secretly believed he, specifically, had been endowed with DNA that allowed him to perform feats well beyond the ordinary. So was the case with Conrad's response to the droughts plaguing the region. He partnered with regional neighbors to create an organization that pumped water from underground sources and stored rainwater to irrigate wide swaths of dry desert surrounding Downey. Financially, the project was, and is, a continuing success. It allowed Conrad to fulfill his marriage agreement and move the family back to the Midwest where Edna could be in closer proximity to her family.

Centralia, Missouri was their chosen destination, after an exhaustive investigation of alternative locations. This was a community still suffering economic decline. The bank had failed along with several local businesses. This made for a gloomy economic future, but Conrad, in keeping with his inherent positive outlook, believed he could stimulate Centralia's economy. He purchased and refurbished four bankrupt retail establishments (the town's only hotel, gas station, automobile and tractor dealerships), and appointed himself, with Edna's assistance, to be the town's only significant lender.

Conrad's aspirations were high but the realities of Centralia's marketplace made them attainable. Historically, potential borrowers offered a wide variety of collateral to secure their loans. According to Edna, most of the collateral (TVs, lawn mowers, sewing machines, wagon wheels, etc.), was antiquated and had little or no market value and represented Conrad's overly solicitous desire to please borrowers. It would fall to Conrad's judgment as to the borrower's capacity and desire to repay the loan, which made the difference in whether or not to lend funds. This was a continuing source of tension between my grandparents, but a functional one. Piles of collateral continued to accumulate, but that did not obscure the fact that Conrad and Edna had generated considerable income. Edna's deep analysis of the prospective borrower's repayment plan as well as Conrad's capacity to instill confidence made them an effective team.

I can personally vouch for this quality of my grandfather's, when as a 15-year-old, I was honored with a direct experience of Conrad's potent encouragement. In the summer of 1950, ready to prove my adulthood, I assisted Conrad with a number of major maintenance projects. We repaired fences and built large silos for storing corn. On foot, we corralled ornery cattle who had trampled down barbwire fences. Conrad kept throwing more at me to do on my own. I found the projects challenging.

I learned to drive his dilapidated, stick-shift, 1948 Dodge pickup truck (relegated to only practice in a fenced-in abandoned pasture). Then the surprise of a 15-year-old's life: Conrad announced at breakfast, that we (Edna, Conrad and I), were going on a holiday in the West, visiting the friends in cities who had been significant in their lives.

I was about to enter the passenger door of a new, four-door Dodge sedan, when Conrad dangled a set of keys in front of me and commanded, "You drive!"

Here we have a 15-year-old – with no driver's license and no driving experience outside of a pasture – being ordered by his grandfather to drive him and his grandmother on a 5,000-mile trip. And I did!

Probably the driving feat would not have happened if it were not for Conrad's silent message to me: "You can do it."

I witnessed and took personal pride in the man who operated a significant portion of the town's commercial real estate and farmland, but his management style and personal being never reflected it. Conrad was always there for me, as he was always there for others, many times to a fault. During the Depression, with the town's bank precariously close to bankruptcy, Conrad become lender-of-last-resort which, because of his unfailing sympathy for the plight of others, almost led to his own financial default. My grandmother Edna is to be thanked for saving the ruin of their assets by intervening to avert the most sizeable and questionable loans that Conrad considered.

EPILOGUE:

Conrad and Edna significantly helped to revitalize Centralia and put the town on a path of continued growth. The two were instrumental in reviving the town's bankrupt bank which took on an increasingly larger share of the town's lending capacity. Conrad was particularly pleased he could assist in this realignment. It allowed him to continue his lending efforts but at a more relaxed pace. With growing personal financial resources at his disposal, he pursued pleasurable activities in new domains.

With Edna's assistance, Conrad organized a trip back to his home in Switzerland where, with the passing of his father, he could reestablish relationships with his brothers and sisters. Travel was first class passage on the Queen Elizabeth going and the Queen Mary returning. Other post-work activities were not necessarily that luxurious but his life was a journey of adventure seasoned with unexpected crises. Retirement was no different, though moderated by his aging.

In 1956, I had the honor of leading Conrad, age 76, out of one of his cornfields, hoe in hand, where he had persisted in chopping weeds strangling his young corn growths. Alzheimer's had taken hold of Conrad to the extent that he only found pleasure in reliving an activity he had found so satisfying in his youth. A short time later, I took him to a hospital in St. Louis, where surrounded by family and friends, he passed away.

SEARCHING FOR MY CONRAD

IT WAS 1972, AND I was 37 years old, on a heritage quest in the tree-draped, winding, single-laned dirt roads of farm country in St. Gallen, Switzerland, just south of the German border. No mountains here. Simply a flat frustrating maze of roads with directions delivered in Schweizerdeutsch, which had little meaning to me. A recent divorce had precipitated a pilgrimage to the Swiss birthplace and childhood home of my paternal grandfather, a place which had been described to me in my youth, but I had never visited, nor had any of my family. The red-sided house and two-story barn resisted identification by local farmers with no appreciation for my English.

If located, this was to be no ordinary visitation to a relative's homestead. Conrad loomed large in my consciousness. He was my hero, my middle-namesake, and the father of my dearly loved and respected father, John Conrad Leader. But it was Conrad's life story and his summer mentorship in my adolescence that inspired me. Subsequently, I realized how much I identified with him. He influenced my aspirations: explore new frontiers, take risks, love heartily, become an entrepreneur of new resources, but in doing so, be attentive to those less fortunate. I hoped I could find renewal and anointing by his spirit from a visit to his birthplace.

As I explored the St. Gallen countryside looking for Conrad's birthplace, his spirit must have been percolating in me. About to give up, a memory trace of Conrad describing a cupola atop the red barn boiled up in my consciousness. The clue allowed the local postmaster to provide precise homing directions to his homesite.

Finally, turning a corner, there it was. "My God, the red two-storied house and cupolaed barn!"

But then, I had a second thought: Is this Conrad's? The postmaster had said the architectural style of both were not necessarily unique in the region.

The only inhabitant in the house was an adolescent girl whose broken English explained that her parents were away in the city. It was unclear if she understood that I, Gerald Conrad Leader, was the grandson of Conrad Leidergerber, who might have lived there - a potential distant relative of hers! She looked confused, but gave me permission to investigate the barn.

Once in the barn, I exclaimed, "This is it!"

French graffiti on the walls, just as Conrad described. Napoleon's soldiers marching South had left their marks. But again a doubt: left only in this barn? Wouldn't soldiers have billeted in every barn and house for kilometers around? Suspicious and disillusioned, I went to my car and was about to back out when the young girl came running from the house and accosted me with a 3 x 3-foot gilded picture frame.

She dusted it off as we studied it on the hood of my car. Photographic portraits of nine stern-faced and unnamed men and women of varying ages, including two priests and three nuns, were arranged in a circle around a photograph of a particularly austere, if not menacing-looking, father and demure mother. The young woman broke my riveted attention to it with the excited waving of an index finger that pointed to the nose of one portrait, and then she literally jabbed mine. My upturned nose, issued generationally to me and my blood offspring by Conrad, could not be confused with the patrician proboscises in this family grouping.

Conrad had been there. He was born and grew up there. He left and lived boldly and generously, a spirit of which I have been inspired to emulate. With my finger caressing Conrad's portrait, I felt a welcome sense of renewal.

DAD'S LEGACY

D<small>AD</small>, M<small>OM</small>, <small>AND</small> I <small>ARE</small> on a Cape Cod beach, picnicking as part of a celebratory weekend. The day before, I had graduated with an MBA in Harvard's 1000-person pulsating Yard. Dad, defying all posted and verbalized announcements, had stood on a well-worn, wooden folding chair and beckoned me for a photograph as I processed by with my classmates. Any embarrassment I felt for his etiquette-breaching behavior was quickly resolved by a warm feeling throughout my body. Dad was demonstratively proud of me.

At the celebratory picnic, Dad pointedly asked me, "Now that you have graduated, what job will you be taking?"

Gratified, I responded, "I've been offered and accepted a place in Harvard Business School's doctoral program with a full-ride scholarship and a monthly financial stipend."

Unexpectedly, Dad exploded. "That is totally ridiculous, giving up all the earning power of your Harvard MBA. This is wasteful and irresponsible!"

I was crushed by his response, and it caught me off-guard. I countered that I had tried to find a job I liked, but nothing was as appealing as the opportunity to teach. I was drawn to the newly emerging field of Organizational Behavior, where, for example, factory workers were given decision-making power and treated as human beings rather than robots.

Dad couldn't understand; he was too angry. When it seemed like his anger had subsided, I repeated my reasoning to join the doctoral program, but he remained convinced that my MBA would not be monetarily leveraged. We were at a stand-off. The celebration denied, we parted on friendly but unresolved terms.

We had never been particularly close. We didn't share common interests or activities; we never spent much time together. But I was shaken. He had never before taken exception to any major decision I had made. My decision remained a source of tension between us, never to be discussed again. Both of us acted as if we had not had the disagreement, but I was left with a bitter aftertaste. This man, my dad, who I had admired and respected couldn't accept my calling. Brought together by subsequent family gatherings, we were happy to see each other, but our relationship had an unspoken fissure.

I knew Dad was justifiably proud, as was I, of his own financial success in the stock and bond market. His skill produced an impressive portfolio which enabled a very comfortable, upwardly mobile lifestyle for our family. With this financial security, he had taken an early retirement from a job he did not enjoy, a middle-level managerial position at the local phone company. His tenure there had been particularly stressful. Arriving there mid-career, he had no experience in coping with a very competitive corporate culture. With only a high school diploma and an entrepreneurial instinct, he had created a modest, independent rural telephone company, which he was forced to sell to Bell, at which time he was obligated to join the company.

In the years following our sad encounter at my MBA graduation, my relationship with Dad remained respectful but unfulfilled. I carried the assumption that Dad did not comprehend the value of my academic, humanistic career path because my compensation was relatively meager. However, my father's appraisal of me changed when I was hired a number of times as an independent corporate consultant in addition to my work at the university.

Monthly, Dad besieged me with a phone call asking, "What is your consulting daily rate, now?"

The repetition was unnerving. Again, I had to monetarily account for my time and efforts. Was Dad so focused on money that a financial metric had to be used in measuring value given and received?

Dad's answer arrived in a most unexpected manner. One weekday morning in October, during a visit home, I interrupted him as he backed out of the garage. He was in the driver's seat of the aforementioned car of his dreams, a shiny Cadillac four-door sedan. He was dressed nattily, in a sports jacket, silk shirt, and shined leather loafers. Where was he going? His outfit and transportation might indicate he was off to a luncheon at the exclusive, members only, Clayton Club. But no, this was when I discovered that Dad was a regular driver in St. Louis's Meals-On-Wheels program, delivering hot meals to incapacitated, homebound people in the city's most economically deprived neighborhoods.

Initially stunned, I couldn't make my picture of Dad whole. The subsequent ride and conversation relieved the dissonance. I cringed, unnerved, as we double-parked, horns blaring in back of us on narrow streets. Dad was as happy as I had ever seen him, whipping out of the car, running up rundown staircases, and eagerly gifting sustenance to his "clients." This practice, which he thoroughly enjoyed, continued until his legs gave out. Dad was sharing the goodness of his life. To this day, I find it a model for being my best self.

SHOUTS AND WHISPERS FROM THE WEST

IN THE SUMMER OF 2002, it hit me. Wren, my 17-year-old son was not ready for the world. He was unfinished. I wasn't done with him. It kept nagging at me; my spell ballooned and finally broke. I held the West responsible.

I was born, raised, and went to college in the Midwest. So, although I have lived most of my life in Boston, my heritage is from the West. I saw myself as a product of the paternal lineage of my grandfather and father, each endowed with a pioneering spirit. I wanted Wren to feel this legacy, and I believed the roots of my clan and the source of this spirit were in Downey, Idaho.

I grew up with stories of my grandparents arriving in Downey in 1910 as newlyweds. With four other couples, they homesteaded and irrigated the arid basin. They helped found the town, and through tilling, irrigating, ranching, butchering, and just plain hard work, made their modest fortune, before retiring to the Midwest. It was that town which nurtured and raised my dad, known to all as Jack. When he left in the early 1930s, he could butcher, farm, and ride, but most significantly, he was prepared to ride tall in the multiple life-saddles that came his way. Downey had blessed him, too, and confidently, he set out to chart new territories.

In 1950, at age 15 (and without a legitimate driver's license), I proudly drove my paternal grandparents to Downey from their home in rural Centralia, Missouri, where I spent my summers. Even though it had been 20 years since they had left, my grandparents returned periodically and still knew everyone in town, and everyone in town knew them.

I was Jack's son, thin as a board, tanned, and constantly wearing a white body-hugging t-shirt, with pompadoured blond hair that would put James Dean to shame. "I sure believe he's taller than Jack," I heard commented. They were proud of me and I was proud to be there. "You say he drove you all the way from Missouri?" I was celebrated, gushed over, looked over, and over fed.

Constantly, I was reminded of my pioneer heritage when walking those streets, smelling the young, sweet wheat in the fields, and hearing the cattle bays echoing from the foothills. Upon leaving Downey in 1950, I stood taller and had a vision of my future, equally adventuresome and as productive as my father's and grandfather's.

In July of 2022, Lucy and I flew to Downey in a small plane. I experienced all the anticipation and feelings that would come from meeting a brother or sister, lost and unknown for half a century. My roots were in that town, along with the place of my coming of age. I carried a secret wish that Downey would be a launching place for Wren. Looking down from 3,000 feet, the town was a gleaming metropolis, ready to receive its long-lost grandson. Shockingly, on the ground it was a ghost town.

Now, Downey was a skeleton of its former self. There were barren, unpaved streets and expanses of sagebrush on city blocks that once held homes, stores, tractor and auto dealerships, harness-makers, livery stables, and friends. Pitifully, the only place for lunch was the Senior Citizen's Center, a cavernous, former dry-goods store, reverberating with the mournful sounds of an octogenarian trio rehearsing Lawrence Welk.

In front of the post office, Fred Collard, in his wheelchair and hard of hearing, reckoned he knew Jack Leader. His recollections were unconvincing, despite my urgent need to believe him. I craved a connection: someone or something to confirm that this was a special place for me, and maybe for my son.

I couldn't stand it. I wanted to get out of town. My heart was desolate as I boarded our plane. I felt disappointed and angry. I had returned to Downey with the hope that this town would give me a vision and energy for

Wren's adult passage. In my mind, I had constructed a paternal totem pole image of Jack, then Gerry, and then Wren, sprung from the shoulders of our fathers. But Downey had failed me. No sacred sites were in sight, just rusted grain silos. This was no place for inspiration. I had to keep looking.

Last spring, when Lucy suggested a family road trip out west to Montana, Utah, and Idaho (along with Wren's friend Sand), I was torn. Possibly, there could be opportunities for Wren to find his way from adolescence to the man he would become. On the other hand, in my darkest moments, I imagined the western landscape peppered with shriveled Downeys. I didn't want to plan the trip. Downey had been a disaster. I would rather let Ouija board vibrations set the course. I longed for a new, beneficent voice from the West. Where would it come from?

Friends suggested, for pure inspiration, an adventure I was strongly in need of: a canoeing and camping trip down the Upper Missouri, following Lewis and Clark's 19th century campsites. Well, alrighty then. Lucy, Wren, Sand, and I would take up the challenge.

The first day was unrelenting. We traveled downstream with the Missouri's steady 8 knots, heading for Lewis and Clark's May 31, 1805, campsite, but headwinds created a 15-knot deficit, calling for my and Lucy's cardiovascular systems, biceps, and triceps, to make up the difference. It was tough going. I was unsure we would make our campsite by nightfall.

As the morning wore on, however, I was more concerned about Wren and Sand, whose canoe had sprinted ahead after our launch. I thought we were supposed to stay in touch. They were nowhere in sight. A hundred ards over our port bow appeared the silhouette of a half-submerged canoe. My terror only relaxed as we got closer and it revealed itself to be driftwood. Ominously, at noon, we passed a shivering family of seven on the bank, obvious products of a capsize. A chill bloated my consciousness, remembering that I had failed Wren as a swimming instructor after repeated summer attempts. He hated treading water and his Australian crawl was labored.

When we finally arrived at Lewis and Clarke's May 31st campsite, it was I who was drowning - in crisscrossed feelings. A feeling of relief wilted my body when I saw Wren and Sand in chest-high water gleefully pitching a Frisbee back and forth. They had arrived hours earlier. I felt a private embarrassment. Finishing the day's trip and pulling the canoe (with Lucy in it), in ankle-deep water, I sadly acknowledged that I didn't have the strength or aptitude to navigate the river. Wren and his companion did. I was stunned as to how much I had underestimated Wren's capacities. The Missouri scolded me. I had projected my own feelings of inadequacy on to Wren. Clearly, I had to keep searching.

A friend, who being raised in the West, understood it, mentioned that we might visit Montana's Big-Hole National Monument on our western odyssey. The national monument, located in southern Montana, memorializes the place where, in 1877, the Nez Perce Tribe valiantly resisted and escaped a savage attack by the U.S. Army. The video at the visitor's center recreated the brutal battle. It was mesmerizing in its uncomfortable clarity depicting the fight.

An hour later, in the dusk of what had been a sunny day, our group followed a meandering path, shaped by the Big-Hole River. Rolling over the grassy hill to our left were low-flying clouds that quite unexpectedly, but presciently, showered us with corn-sized hail nuggets. Completing this introductory overture was a mile-wide rainbow unfolding through the clouds drifting to our right. Something big was about to happen. Looking forward, 20 skeleton teepees (just the poles attached at the top), commanded the meadow.

Wren had walked ahead into the center of the encampment and I saw him silhouetted against the fading rainbow and encroaching sunset. Why were his hands covering his eyes? Was he grieving?

In my mind, Wren became the warrior "Looking Glass," the one charged by Chief Joseph to protect the tribe from a surprise attack. In my imaginings, he had let his guard down. The encampment was being ravaged by U.S. Army regulars. How could I have let him become so irresponsible?

And where was I in this episode? Of the over 20 characters in the drama of the battle, painstakingly researched by the Nez Pierce in collaboration with the U.S. Army, I transposed Wren into "Looking Glass," a person ill-prepared for his responsibilities. It was a stunning transposition to make and a self-revealing transposition for me to see. Who really was the delinquent one?

I gave up my quest for answers on whether or not Wren was ready for manhood; it had been futile. The question kept boomeranging and pointing to me. Our vacation moved on from Montana to Idaho, then to Utah. Ten days later, we were astride mules riding in a majestic canyon. Kenny Hall, who bred, broke, trained, sold, and rode mules, horses, and ornery bulls, was our guide. A waitress in Doug's Restaurant and General store in Bryce volunteered that Kenny was a real cowboy. A holdover from another era. He was not a four-wheel, all-terrain jockey. It was not an easy life, but one he had crafted. When not working at the Forest Service, he was raising his son Landon to ranch, ride, and rope.

As we made our way through the expansive Utah scenery, Kenny, mounted on one of his most accomplished steeds, turned in his saddle. He told us that mules, in the canyon's terrain, were like sherpas in the Himalayas: you wouldn't want to be without one.

We roamed the back corridors of uncharted Escalante National Monument. The stage for this wandering journey was a dry, school bus-wide riverbed, sometimes 8 feet deep, interrupting scrub pines and brush. Sure enough, the nimble-footed mules navigated the uneven matrix of nature's random impediments with the ease of an Olympic slalom skier on the way to gold.

Perhaps the divining rod strategy of our trip and believing in the omnipresent but unobservable that guided our trip, succeeded in pointing my stick at Kenny. A day later, it worked out for me to take a solo mule excursion with him.

Our ride was peppered with an intermittent, walkie-talkie-like conversation, occasioned by our mules finding separate paths through the maze of bushes. To my astonishment, the mules would independently power glide down a steep riverbank. Like AOL's "Instant Messenger," the soundbites allowed an intimate sharing of personal history to develop between Kenny and me that probably would have embarrassed us, if we had been speaking face-to-face.

"Never been East, must be hard to get around in Boston, I've heard," he said, followed by: "You say Downey, Downey, Idaho?

I'll be damned. I used to date a girl from there. Went to high school in Preston, 20 miles north."

What did he say? He knew Downey? He'd been there! He knew my family's hometown. It turned out that Preston, where Kenny had lived, was as dried up as Downey, but he escaped, let go, and moved on. There was a new life and wife for him in Escalante.

After our ride, Kenny said he would be singing at Doug's, if we were planning to eat there. I was stunned. This wrangler and rodeo rider Kenny was going to sing for us! After the initial surprise wore off, it seemed too much to believe. This was the script of a 1950s Roy Roger's film: a ride on the range and, as a closer, a singing and strumming cowboy.

Sure enough, Lucy, Wren, and I ate at Doug's that evening, and in strode Kenny Hall. Showered from the afternoon's ride, he wore a freshly-pressed western shirt, and a coffee-saucer-sized buckle, announcing his national championship as a bull rider. Kenny poked Lem (the evening's singer taking a break), on either side of Lem's considerable girth, playfully demanded his pick, and proceeded to the microphone with Lem's guitar.

Kenny's original song, "Sweet Voice of Freedom," has stayed with me over the years. We were different men from different cultures, but father-to-father, we were kindred spirits.

He'll be no longer fixin' fences,
Once he's seen riding old Cheyenne.

The rancher schemes to change his dreams,
Calls his cowboy to stay this way.

But daddy knows he has to let him go,
Let him spread his wings and fly.

I had come full circle, from Downey to Kenny Hall and back. The West had finally spoken, and I could listen.

Epilogue: The Modern-day Cowboy

On January 2nd 2004, Wren and I finished a two-day, father and son road trip in his 1989 Camry and arrived in Detroit, Michigan, via Canada's Windsor tunnel. He drove, I navigated, miserably. I directed us to at least four wrong turns, and we got completely lost twice. I flew back; Wren was on his own, living with an unfamiliar couple in gritty Detroit. He was on a two-month-long, winter internship at a rapper's recording studio, where Eminem was known to rhyme.

Wren did quite well. He pumped his first gas, made his first ATM withdrawal, and quite easily found his way around the Detroit freeways and for that matter...in life. In February, he drove by himself from Detroit to his college in Bennington, Vermont. In April, he drove himself to New York and scurried up Madison Avenue to pick up his uncle for a lunch date in Harlem. How's that for moving out?

Dad has let go.

MENTORS

DEAN STRIDER

USUALLY, THE INFLUENCE OF A host of lifetime mentors was unintentional. We crossed paths and our intersection resulted in explosive consequences. I gasp at the thought of who and where I would be today without these relationships. Their faces populate my personal Mt. Rushmore. This chapter honors another of my life-altering, pop-up mentors to whom I am soulfully grateful.

My alma mater, Maplewood Richmond Heights High School, located in a working-class suburb of St. Louis was tough. Little value was given to academics. Sports had to be your calling, of which I was particularly unsuited. My life course seemed to hold little promise of providing a secure foothold in the middle class.

In response, my parents shipped me off to Camp Minnewonka, a Christian leadership camp on the northern shores of Lake Michigan, in hopes the experience might alter the path I was traveling. My baggage included not only two pairs of Converse sneakers, but a strong desire to prove I could finally qualify as one of the boys at my high school.

Boy, did that decision impact me.

Unlike my high school classmates, I was off to an out-of-state university, Iowa State College of Agriculture and Mechanical Arts. We were known colloquially as the shit kickers. When I started engineering classes, I couldn't quite believe I was pushing numbers and solving equations. How did I get here? Mentorship by Mrs. Bartlett, the Home Economics teacher at my high school was a strong factor. She happened to also be the chief cook at Camp Minnewonka, and she hired and trained me as a soup chef. She counseled me to go to college, even though my grades were only so-so. Mrs. Bartlett insisted engineering was coming of age in 1953, and I had an A- in algebra. So, I had applied and was accepted.

However…at Iowa State, the more I got into it, the more I knew engineering wasn't for me. I considered delivering prayers to a committed student flock as my preferred alternative. On Sunday mornings, the campus came alive. Everybody went to church. Streams of students left dormitories and filed to their respective denominational places of worship. A relatively meager and spotty Sunday school record back home blossomed into what I thought was true believer status. Sunday mornings at First Presbyterian were a reverie for imagining myself delivering the Word to an appreciative congregation.

Over several months, Reverend Rimley listened to my new career aspirations, but offered only modest comments. Frustrated by his meager replies, I asked, "Should I go to divinity school?"

Much to my surprise and delight, he invited me to deliver the morning prayer and followed with, "You will know."

Anxious to please, I scoured books of prayers to find the most eloquent. I stood in the high pulpit of the Ames, Iowa, Presbyterian church basking in the warmth of the 300 or so smiling faces of student parishioners below me. I enjoyed the regal persona I projected with a black robe accentuated by a magenta stole around my neck. My efforts were well received although I felt increasingly sheepish that I was borrowing someone else's work.

Then one rainy morning, I read and prayed, "We trust you, our heavenly Father, to lead us in paths of sin…oh no, no, lead us in paths of righteousness, you know, righteousness." Pause.

The congregation jerked their heads up and fixed their eyes on me. Perspiration enveloped me. I wadded up my paper and said, "You know it's paths of righteousness. Amen."

And they echoed 'Amen' giving a final chorus to not only the prayer, but to my career as a preacher. Embarrassed and yet relieved, I stumbled through the rest of the service and met with Reverend Rimley that afternoon.

With a forgiving smile and a warm handshake, he said, "Now we know."

He suggested, and I accepted, an invitation to give an original prayer the following Sunday. At the service, if etiquette would have allowed it, I'm sure the parishioners would have clapped after hearing my apology for the previous Sunday's word debacle.

After the service, the pit in my stomach grew daily. No preaching, no engineering for me. How would I tell Dean Strider that I was withdrawing from his prized department?

I finally got up the courage to meet with him. I explained my dilemma, my voice, raised by an octave.

Dean Strider's response left me humbled. "Gerry, you have worked hard, but engineering, let's face it, is not for you. You are a leader; you are president of this, VP of that. Weren't you VP of the Union Board? And I hear you are ROTC Regimental Commander. You are going to the Harvard Business School! That is, when you finish your army commitment. Write me a letter, and I'll write you a superlative recommendation, and you will be accepted.

At the time, I didn't know the Harvard Business School from Future Farmers of America. Not trusting my own judgment and having no necessary sense of direction, I took his advice. If Dean Strider said it was my destiny, that was good enough for me.

MASTER SERGEANT CHARLES J. MARCEL

IT'S NOVEMBER, 1957. A MONTH earlier I had been assigned as a U.S. Army Second Lieutenant, commander of an infantry company responsible for the training of 220 draftees at Fort Leonard Wood, Missouri. My position was typically held by an officer of captain rank and some 10-15 years my senior, but the number of captains had been seriously depleted in the Korean War. In its infinite wisdom and desperation, the Pentagon was taking newly-minted second lieutenants from University ROTC programs and with only two months of officer training, assigning them to positions well beyond their level of experience and formal preparation. I was one of them. So, I was supposed to train infantrymen, but I had never been one or seen one, except in Hollywood movies.

My ranking NCO (Non-Commissioned Officer), Master Sergeant Charles J. Marcel, provided an introduction to the Company: who was who and where is what - at my Company headquarters, a weather beaten, leaking, two-room, wood-framed building, vintage early 1940s.

One afternoon, a knock at the door is answered by Master Sergeant Marcel and in march two military policemen, and two Black NCOs who I recognize as being part of my command. My first emotional response: I'm stunned and angry. I dismiss the MP's and usher the two NCOs into my office and seat them in front of my desk. The MP's written report told of the two being picked up, each with delinquent two-day passes to be outside the boundary of the fort. Their justification for an unauthorized two-day absence was flimsy and quite suspect.

I was mad. I felt I was being scammed because I was a newcomer, and I was winding up to tell them so, but looked up and saw Master Sergeant Marcel watching me through the half-open door between his office and mine. He was short, stocky, and balding, with intense green eyes that wouldn't leave me alone. His almost imperceivable, left to right, right to left head motion immobilized me and my vocal cords. The two NCOs don't see Master Sergeant Marcel; he is behind them; they are facing forward. They must have been mystified by my abrupt halt and awkward verbal recovery. I dismiss them and command they return the following day.

Master Sergeant Marcel apologized for not having the opportunity earlier to explain the circumstances of their tardy return to the fort. He, too, was surprised at the timing of the MP's bringing the NCO's back to our headquarters, and went on to share their story.

Each of the two Black NCOs are married to White women. The couples had tried to live in the fort's NCO married housing, but had been unmercifully harassed because of their mixed-race coupling. Their wives had to move back to their family homes in Chicago, some 440 miles from Fort Leonard Wood. They could not accumulate enough leave time to have regular round trip visits home to see their wives. In response, Master Sergeant Marcel had arranged undisclosed schedules to allow them more time in Chicago. But this secret scheduling put Master Sargent Marcel, the two NCOs, and now myself, as co-complicitors in potential jeopardy of disciplinary action if the schedule were to be revealed to fort authorities. Either I blow up the conspiracy now, and have the three disciplined, or join the arrangement and risk disciplinary action for the four of us at some future date. I had only spent two weeks working with Master Sargent Marcel, but his humanity and personal integrity were evident daily. If he thought making the lives of the two NCOs substantially more agreeable at some small risk to us, I would join him.

This was not the last time I followed Master Sergeant Marcel's lead. He became my behind-the-scenes mentor and I the beneficiary of this wise and humble man's council. He, who had been part of the first allied unit to liberate Amsterdam from the Nazis at the end of WWII, would give almost an extra quarter of his workday to training a 22-year-old neophyte in the art of command. It was accomplished surreptitiously so as not to embarrass me as was true with his discrete headshaking "no" in my office when the two NCOs were about to receive my full wrath.

Master Sergeant Marcel's tough lessons were always at the ready. On a nighttime maneuver, I had led my 220 soldiers down the wrong path at a three-way intersection, substantially extending their march. I believed there was no need to confess the mistake. They might never have realized it was a longer journey, but Master Sergeant Marcel counseled owning the mistake and informing the troops why and how I had made it.

Master Sergeant Marcel will forever be in my memory. His spirit of generosity and integrity was a model that I hold sacred.

DAN TROOP SMITH – TOUGH LOVE

WITH MY NEWLY ACQUIRED HARRIS Tweed sport jacket; button down, oxford cloth shirt; and brightly striped, silk rep tie, I proudly stride into Aldrich Hall, along with 900 Harvard Business School classmates, similarly garbed. I am at the mecca for business leadership in 1959. They are going to make me a leader.

My bloom quickly wilted, more accurately dissolved. Iowa State's engineering curriculum, without a single English course, was not intended as a prep and failed me as a tune up for Harvard Business School. Weekly papers came back covered in red graffiti. Students were red meat for each other. The 90 classmates in my cohort were primed to annihilate each other's classroom contributions.

The coliseum opened its gate every morning at 8 am. Professor Dan Troop Smith of wiry thin physique and narrowly sculpted face, displayed a verbal rapidity that left little doubt that he had, indeed, the requisite smarts to almost singlehandedly write the U.S. 1954 tax code.

"Mr. Leader, President Sarnoff looks at the most recent quarterly income statement of Sarnoff Industries: profits are deteriorating precipitously. If you were he, what would you do?"

All of us had read the Sarnoff case the night before. I was the randomly chosen target of Smith's opening salvo. My classmates were relieved, now at a competitive advantage as I trailed out my response. They savaged it, championing their own. It was verbal fisticuffs, but apparently, if you're going to be a business leader, this was the required boot camp. It was not for me. After two months, I decided to pack my bags.

To withdraw, the registrar required a visit to Assistant Dean Shepley Saltonstall. At that time, 1959, he is the one administrator for 1800 students sent for counseling. Saltonstall had a reputation of having mentored some of HBS's greats, an aspiration which at the time was far from my reach.

Not five seconds into Dean Saltonstall's office, holding what could only be my academic record, he whirled around to face me.

"Damn, Leader, you should never have left Ames, the best nine west of the Mississippi."

I'm flummoxed. What does he mean 'nine' in Ames? Nine courses? No need to ponder. For the next 20 minutes, Dean Saltonstall wages through every hole, approach, sand trap, and putting green tilt of Ames Iowa's golf course.

Finally, he says, "Back to Ames, my boy. May Ben Hogan be your guide. Oh, by the way, let Dan Troop Smith know you're leaving."

My trudge to Smith's office had all the effect of a gallows walk. My feeble knock at his door was answered within seconds by a hurried invitation for me to sit down, followed by a rapid-fire query.

"Do you think Watson had enough capital to safely launch IBM's 360?" Smith was already into the IBM case assigned for the following day.

I admitted I hadn't read the case and stumbled through my withdrawal story.

His staccato reply was rapid and curt. "You are not doing any such thing. You will write a case analysis of three double-spaced pages with two pages of appendices, handed to me at the beginning of class. You will participate in the class discussion, and I will give you written feedback. You will do this every class day until the end of the semester. Now, go back and tell me whether Mr. Watson was brave or foolish and why."

That I did and did it again and again until the final exam which earned Harvard Business School's equivalent of an A. Dan Troop Smith changed my life. With the approval of other instructors, I spread his feedback-learning model to the rest of my courses and graduated with my MBA in June, 1961.

Yes, I graduated with several elective courses in organizational behavior under my belt and a heightened sense of self-confidence, belief that I had the right stuff to be a leader. But where could I practice leadership? Jobs in industry didn't interest me: teaching leadership did. That was the reason I entered Harvard Business School's doctoral program, which subsequently catapulted me into a 40-year career at Stanford, Harvard, Tulane, and Boston University in preparing graduate business students to be more effective managers. Thank you, Professor Smith.

RALPH LANGLEY AND
HARVARD BUSINESS SCHOOL

THE EARLY 1960S SAW ME at the Harvard Business School pursuing an MBA and subsequently a doctorate. My goal was to perfect my then good, but not great, leadership in the service of a well-paying corporate position. That objective was up-ended when I met Ralph Langley, a most unlikely person to change the trajectory of my leadership quest.

Ralph made his entrance via an HBS case study discussed in class, in which he was the featured leader. My classmates were indifferent, but I was dumbfounded and exhilarated. Ralph, an electronics manufacturing plant manager, had taken a sullen, disgruntled and particularly low-performing group of 20 and catapulted them into a collaborative team where each went out of their way to assist the others and the team to achieve record productivity. He did it without more pay or offering more perks. I had never read of such a marvel. The guy was a genius. In part, my motivation to enter the doctoral program following my MBA was to study Ralph and Ralphs like him and deliver their leadership message to the uninitiated.

I had to meet this guy and learn how he did it. Admitted to the factory floor on my first visit, I had trouble finding Ralph. He seemed to blend in.

When I did, Ralph exploded all of my preconceptions of a leader. The handshake was mushy, voice barely audible, dressed in greasy coveralls at least two sizes too large for his frail, stoop-shouldered frame.

I explained why I was visiting and asked, "How did you do it? How did you motivate your team?"

"It's not me you want to talk to. Ask Mike, Charlie, Mildred, ask them."

I do.

Mildred's response is fairly representative. "Ralph thinks I know more than he does, and when I run into trouble, I know where to go. And he's right about that. We are pretty damn good. Have you seen the chart? Not bad. We push each other. Yeah, sometimes, one of us will take a dive but there's always Jack or Charlie to pick you up. Ralph's our back up."

The team leading the way and the leader backing them up was an over-simplified model of leadership, but to me it was revolutionary. I had to know more, and I did in the Harvard Business School's doctoral program. I learned that leadership was a far more complex topic, but my takeaway was that corporations were vastly underutilizing the exponential potential of their employees. It was there, but it took enlightened leaders to tap the human capital for the benefit of the individual and the organization. This message, destined for thousands of MBA candidates across four universities, put fire in my belly and sustained a teaching career for over 50 years.

Peter Gabriel – Testing Fate

WHEN I LOOK BACK ON my career at Boston University, I am struck by how random, brief interactions with people have had such powerful consequences; how little seeds of conversation or tiny events could evolve into lasting relationships. I'm on the lookout for the seemingly innocuous connections which can energize power to change lives and institutions. I've been on both ends of these types of experiences.

Let me set the stage. My career prior to BU was quite problematic with several short appointments at Stanford, Harvard, and Tulane. I couldn't seem to alight more than two to five years in any one place. I won teaching awards, but my scholarly production was minimal.

When working at Tulane University in New Orleans, I was awarded tenure based upon excellent teaching, but I achingly wanted to move back to Boston where my two daughters lived. On an Eastern Airlines, non-stop flight from New Orleans to Boston for a visit, I sat comfortably with my morning coffee, and when I glanced up, a man was bearing down on me with bulldozer determination. My mind raced. Is he heading for me? He looked faintly familiar, but who was he? Before I could compose an answer, he was on me.

"It's you," he says. "You're Gerry, Gerry Leader. I'll never forget you. You gave me an unsatisfactory in Lombard's Interpersonal Relations course."

Bang. Sure enough, he had me. While a doctoral student at Harvard Business School, I was a teaching assistant. I had given Peter Gabriel, the future Dean of Boston University's Business School, the lowest grade he had ever received in his academic career. His confrontation with me suggested he hadn't internalized major portions of the course. Apparently, that hadn't mattered to John Silber, who unilaterally appointed him Dean of Boston University's Business School.

Fortunately, Peter didn't hold grudges, and like his boss, John Silber, Peter delighted in being confrontational and decisive. On the remainder of the flight to Boston, he offered me a visiting professorship at BU and the opportunity to be Chair and carve out a separate OB Department from the then departmental amalgam of Marketing, Strategy, and OB. I accepted Peter's offer, conditional on my Tulane tenure translating to tenure at BU, but started the visiting gig at BU while things were sorted.

The university said nothing-doing. If I wanted to extend my professorship at Boston University, I would have to go through the tenure process. My case was problematic at best and most likely doomed, but I reluctantly applied. Nothing happened for months until a bitterly cold January afternoon. I was running, very late to my 1 o'clock class on the third floor of 685 Commonwealth Avenue. "Dammit." I said under my breath. Worse still, I was supposed to meet a student before class.

Flushed with embarrassment and breathing heavily, I burst through the back door of the sixty-degree classroom and leapt to the front podium. My peripheral vision picked up a rumpled figure of a man huddled in a dark overcoat slumped in the furthest corner of the classroom. Should I kick him out? It would make quite a scene. I'd deal with him later.

Emotionally aroused, I led a premium discussion, if I do say so, of a case that I had written and practiced a number of times. Afterwards, the students filed out and the phantom figure stumbled to his feet.

He extended his hand. "Braxton McGuire. I will send you a copy of my report."

I raced to my office and started phoning. This was before Google. Who in the hell was Braxton? What was his name, McGuire? It turned out he was a university professor of philosophy of international fame and a hand-picked ally of John Silber. I thought Boston University was through with me, and I had started to pack my bags to return to New Orleans, when a copy of his tenure report landed on my desk. According to him, I had taken the mundane aspects of administrative pragmatics and lifted them to new heights of intellectual discourse. I thought the hyperbole was embarrassingly disingenuous, but it gave me safe passage into the halls of Boston University for the next thirty years.

I was a little dumbfounded. How had that happened? Oblique connections with Peter and Braxton had come along at just the right time to change the course of my personal, family, and career history.

ROGER, LUCY, AND GERRY

BEGINNING IN APRIL, 2021 AND extending into September, 2022, my wife, Lucy, and I witnessed a male Osprey (who I named Roger), attempt to build a nest atop a decayed wooden pole. It had once held an Osprey birding platform, but now the platform was gone. The 10-foot pole was stuck in the tidewater pond at a 45-degree angle. Roger, repeatedly, would craft an exquisite, interwoven nest of twigs and branches only to have it slide down the pole after a rain or windstorm. Over and over, again and again, always with the same result, the nest crashed into pieces at the bottom of the pole. But Roger's quest for fatherhood was not deterred. He would start over again at the top of the pole.

During this time, Roger and I developed a relationship. On hikes near Roger's construction, we made eye contact. He seemed to recognize my empathy. He knew I was with him.

Then, Roger stopped. Daily he stood motionless, a silent martyr to a fatherless life. His stoicism was broken by his flying up to my fourth-floor tower window and perching himself not 2 feet away from me. I was startled but not surprised. Roger raised his wings for my attention, shook them and looked me directly in the eyes. I was not to give up on him. He would be back!

Three days later, following our conversation, Roger abandoned his perch and flew away. He was probably participating in the Ospreys' September migration to South or Central America. Lucy and I were saddened by his leaving before he had the opportunity to fulfill his life's mission: fatherhood and the propagation of his species. We asked ourselves: Was there anything we could do?

Would Roger return and if so, where would he build his nest? His nemesis -- the 45-degree slanted pole -- appeared to have an unrelenting attraction for Roger even though it could no longer embrace a nest longer than the next rain storm. We couldn't let Roger be consumed by this wicked pole.

In late March of 2022, when Osprey start their migration back to the states from South America, Lucy secretly commissioned the construction of an aluminum nesting platform, 3 feet in diameter, and mounted on a new10-foot post to be located in the exact spot where the older pole had been cut down.

The new platform and its location were designed to be the ultimate Roger attractor. Osprey parents are known to value having their offspring born where they themselves had been given life. Might that explain why Roger was so obsessively persistent in trying to build a nest on the old pole, and could the new platform and post be a very attractive alternative?

In early April, Roger was not to be denied the prize which had been prepared for him. Swooping in and fighting off rivals with aerial acrobatics, he took possession of the new platform. Immediate nest-building established it was his. Beware competitors. Lucy and I were jubilant!

Roger's committed nest construction would hopefully fulfill an innate purpose: the attraction of a female. DNA wired Osprey females to be particularly attracted to intricately woven assemblages of sticks and branches. Roger's nesting productions were of this character, and he was inundated with prospective mates. Sophia (who I also named), was ingenious in winning Roger's attention and ultimately their life-long partnership. Although uninvited, she had snuggled herself next to him in the nest-building process. Roger would be a father.

Sophia and Roger were as intricate with their parenting as Roger had been with his nest building. With their chick, named Bourne by Lucy, they demonstrated a tough love strategy: soothing caresses and withholding the food when Bourne was particularly belligerent. At our last viewing, Bourne sat alone, regally erect but now reliant on personal ingenuity without parental backup. Roger and Sophia had departed - from a home whose construction we were proud to have been a part of.

WATCHING ALICIA

EVOLVING BEYOND CHILDHOOD, MID-WESTERN PREJUDICES have been important in my life journey. So, during the winter before COVID, I, along with seven or eight other volunteers for social justice from First Parish Brookline and twenty undocumented immigrants, were at Chelsea's non-profit Collaborativo. We were stuffing Spanish-language inserts into Chelsea's weekly newspaper for distribution to all Spanish-speaking Chelsea residents. The inserts described the legal rights of undocumented immigrants and what to do when confronted or possibly arrested by U.S. Department of Immigration, ICE agents.

The early morning preparatory meeting prior to our departure was like a Latin festival, filled with inspirational speeches, Latin food, singing and dancing. Tortilla chips and donut crumbs littered the floor. This social justice experience took me and my fellow-churchgoers into a culture different from our own. I felt energized but was confused by the seeming lack of organization. I didn't know how I could be helpful, what could I do? There was no talk of how we were going to do the distribution. I searched for clarification from the Collaborativo's director but was interrupted by a shout of: "Let's go!" So, I joined the group holding paper bags filled with inserted newspapers, spilling out onto Chelsea's main street.

One of the volunteers appeared to know where to go, and I followed her, bringing up the rear of the pack. Then someone shouted, "Alicia, go with him." Turning around, I saw a short, middle-aged, Latina volunteer with a seriously disabled leg, cane in hand, negotiating the icy sidewalks. My offer to assist her around a particularly large snow pile was refused with a sweeping hand rebuke.

The pack proceeded ahead of us, and I was concerned that we'd get left behind. Alicia forged ahead on her own, attempting to climb steep steps to deliver the inserted newspapers, but my being 85 years old made it hard for each of us. Alicia backed off from the apartment buildings and continued to hobble up the street. I followed her. No talking or even gestures passed between us.

She ended up standing alone, supported by her cane at a bus stop at one of Chelsea's busiest intersections. I felt bewildered. I stood 20 feet behind her and didn't know what to do.

A bus pulled up and Alicia confronted a Latino rider stepping off by thrusting a newspaper into his hand. Surprised, he surveyed it while Alicia delivered a rapid-fire Spanish message. A nod, then he walked off with the newspaper. The scenario repeated 10 or 15 times, exhausting Alicia's supply of the important missives. She turned her head and made eye contact, the first recognition I had received from her.

I finally got it! I ran up and delivered my bag of newspapers to her. Still no talking, but her unexpected, generous smile enveloped me. I felt relieved and filled with joy. Together we went back to the Collaborativo for more insert-laden newspapers and coffee. Without a word spoken, we transcended the cultural language barrier, then returned to the bus stop in partnership and delivered inserted newspapers the rest of the afternoon.

AN ODE TO MY MUSE, SOPHIA LOREN

THIS IS A STORY WHICH contains all the elements of the improbable, at least on first hearing. But to me, as the witness and recorder, the event caused me to question the limits in known physics of the connections between the seemingly random events of our lives.

In one sense, this tale both starts and ends on an early Saturday morning in first class; pardon me, on Alitalia it is called "Magnifica," on a Boeing 747, Flight 2211 to Rome from New York's Kennedy Airport. It begins innocently...

I'm seated comfortably in my leather-padded airline bark-a-lounger, being pampered by a chief steward who won't let either my gastronomic nor libational needs go unfulfilled. I'm an airborne king for half a day.

Having savored the proffered final Rosa wine selection, the cabin lights are dimmed and there, not four feet away on a silver screen, in life-sized proportions, is Sophia Loren. Beguiling and impetuous, she is mischievously romancing the socks, if not the pants, off of Marcello Mastroianni in the 1960s film, *Marriage Italian Style*.

How did Alitalia know to book this film for *this* flight? How did I wind up on *this* flight (more to come on this question)? The film feels like an integral part of my own story. The plot line is pretty simple, but its meaning to me and seeing the film at this moment is an extraordinary event.

Mastroianni is a rich playboy who falls in love with an impoverished but gorgeous call girl, Loren. He establishes her as his unwedded "wife" to manage his household and the family business, while he is off seeking other amorous adventures. After 20 years of this arrangement, the ever-dramatic and resourceful Sophia (with the help of household servants and the village padre and doctor), tricks Mastroianni into marrying her. She fakes a fatal illness and guilts him into matrimony as her final death bed request. When she arises from the "dead" - immediately after the simple ceremony - she breaks the secret that she is the mother of three sons, one of whom is his.

When I initially saw the film (upon its release), the contest of wills that resulted turned out to be one of my most powerful experiences in emotional education. Among the many Sophia lessons that I took away from her tutelage, were:

It's okay to be angry, better the makeup.

To live passionately is to live.

Making love is not just a matter of bodies and positions, but rather plumage, the chase, resistance, and relinquishing.

Honestly, I absorbed this instruction deeply and it truly impacted how I interacted with romantic partners throughout my life.

Let me put this in context with a little relevant, personal history. All of my children and grandchildren walk around with little pug noses, genetically engineered by my paternal Swiss grandfather, who most assuredly came from the German side of that small, multi-ethnic country.

For many years, I took particular pride in my heritage that gave significantly high priority to the values of order, efficiency, cleanliness, and punctuality. I used to brag to my childhood friends that I was 50 percent Swiss and the other half German, and Switzerland was the country where they made the best watches and their trains ran on time. In some misguided career aspiration, prompted by a moderate aptitude for mathematics, I attended engineering school and upon graduation, I designed jets and non-functioning missiles for Boeing aircraft in Seattle.

Ultimately, my need for structure and logic dissipated, as it became clear that those values could not sustain nor even create a satisfying life. My heart/soul/being yearned for something more. After a six-year apprenticeship at Harvard to learn how to be verbally and analytically smart, I moved west. In the 1960s, this earnest and somewhat stolid Midwesterner was trying to make sense of the completely outrageous counter culture of California. Offbeat and foreign movies were an integral part of the scene and became a private guide to a new way of thinking and acting. And, did I need help! Here was a 30-year-old, socialized in the middle 50's in the collegiate courtship practices of Iowa State College of Engineering and Agricultural Arts, thrust into a completely new dating game where diving into the sack on the first date was deemed standard practice.

My first exposure to a non-Rock Hudson/Doris Day Hollywood film didn't help my manly self-confidence. It was man-eating Jane Fonda 'piranha-ing' her way through Barbarella. Viagra was nowhere in sight - not for me, nor the poor male souls who Jane tested.

On the other hand, my first foreign film, *It Started in Naples*, was an entirely different matter. Clearly, the marquee star was Clark Gable, but it was his little-known co-star, Sophia Loren, with whom I started a life-long infatuation. She became my fantasized, more experienced, older woman who would guide me through the treacherous maze of the 60s. I like to think I lost my emotional virginity with Sophia Loren. When she won the Oscar for best actress in *Two Women*, it validated my choice of who to put my faith in for a good model for how to live and love passionately.

I told you that this story starts and ends with my being in the first-class cabin of Flight 2211, but that's not completely true. The eerie thing really started three weeks prior to the flight when I pledged that I wasn't going to stay up and watch the Academy Awards; after all, it was a weeknight! Lucy and Jody might indulge in gown gossip and be taken in by such Hollywood manufactured hype, but I had better things to do.

But…I did stay up and watch, for what reason remains a mystery.

There was something premeditated about the wonderfully talented, Italian actor, Roberto Benigni walking over seats and people when his Oscar for *Life is Beautiful* was announced. You couldn't help but be emotionally exhilarated for him. But the flash, visceral tightening of my stomach was not due to watching his antics. These feelings arose from being unexpectantly confronted with the presence, after many years, of a former hot girlfriend. I hadn't been prepared for my reaction when TV cameras, just a few moments before, had followed the slow, stately, samba-like walk of Sophia Loren to the microphone. There she was after 30 years: my Sophia. It was as if the cameraperson knew my connection, because the picture on the screen lingered on her graceful entrance capturing every curve and fold of her Armani gown as it undulated and squeezed her silhouette, which had not decayed one bit after 40 years.

At the time, I was unaware of the connections to come, but clearly, atoms were aligning themselves in ways that, in another application, would have been capable of an atomic blast.

Lucy, Wren, and I had not been booked first class on Flight 2211 from New York to Rome. We'd been booked economy, steerage class from Boston to Milan, transferring to a flight from Milan to Rome.

Unfortunately, we experienced a frustrating start to our Roman holiday to visit the contingent of my family located in Italy (Nicola, Michela, Emily, and Kristin). We became uncharacteristically snarled in traffic in the Ted Williams tunnel on the way to Logan Airport.

Now that I think about it, that should have been the first clue that things would go amiss. The tunnel would've been named for Babe Ruth, if a greedy Red Sox owner hadn't traded the Bambino, as he was called, evoking his Italian heritage, to the Yankees in 1927. The traffic jam was the curse of the Bambino visiting itself, but in this instance, for the good.

An hour late for our check-in, the flight had been overbooked and Alitalia was loath to unseat any passengers. Instead, they used the inducement of a financial incentive and free ticket to pare the passenger list down. They started to book alternative flights for us and the 20 or so other passengers who had lost seats in their game of musical chairs.

Lucy handles our family travel negotiations, and she is good at it. If weren't for her, Alitalia would've booked us (like the 20 lambs who accepted their options without even a Baa), on a convoluted itinerary where economy was not only the class of booking, but their main fin ancial objective. They were sending people to Rome via New Hampshire, Ontario, and Brussels; that is, once they got themselves back to the airport the next morning.

It was either providence or Lucy's skills, or both, that got us the first-class upgrades on Flight 2211 from Kennedy to Rome. The arm waving and gesturing Alitalia ticket agents were completely nonplussed when Lucy stepped over the baggage scales to the back of the counter and went directly to the airline's holiest of holiest, the supervisor's office, and returned with our Magnifica class tickets to Rome.

Meanwhile, I'm waiting in the lounge area with Wren who is continuing his own love affair, in this instance with Star Trek. And there, laying on the seat next to me is Clue No. 2, a discarded copy of the academy awards issue of *People* magazine. On the cover, with square-inch coverage equal to the starlets one third of her age, is my Sophia.

So far, it was simply a coincidence that I had recently seen Sophia on a TV and in a magazine. We were transported to Kennedy via an air shuttle, and because of our new status, were directed to Alitalia's first class Magnifica lounge. Immediately, we were engulfed in a preparatory bath of upper-class Italian culture: a loudly snorting padre, a self-service espresso machine, and assorted designer-clothed passengers who could afford the 10 million lire first class plane ticket.

Of course, the flight had been delayed. It was 4 a.m., Saturday morning, and we were mid-Atlantic before Marriage Italian Style reached its climax. I am barely aware of where I am, how I got there, and who else is with me. Sophia and Marcello have taken me on a psychic memory trip. If I didn't know better, I would've thought drug-induced. They were fighting, throwing, pleading, pouting, posturing, and sprawling in the roadside dirt before they relinquished their pride and madly folded into a passionate kiss and embrace.

I'm in it; it's like an emotional graduation test. Could I keep up with Sophia as she dishes out her full repertoire of feelings? Thirty years ago, probably not, but at least now, in my own mind, I pass. It's exhilarating, even if it's a vicarious exchange through the medium of a movie. I have my close encounter of an emotional kind with Sophia and, to top it off, I do it when she's at her best.

The final scene of the movie unfolds. Sophia, having married Marcello a second time (this time clearly for the long haul), allows herself a good cry, something she had withheld throughout the emotionally turbulent intervening years.

I'm tearing up, too. The first-class compartment is silent and motionless. Practically everyone is asleep and the once bustling flight attendants, having not anticipated the film's ending, are nowhere in sight. Slightly embarrassed by my emotional response and without a Kleenex, I blot my eyes with my sleeve. As I turn to go back aft and lower my arm, I'm stunned and initially disbelieving.

Four rows behind me, nestled into the back of the compartment, are *THE* almond eyes, also freshly moist, unexpectedly focused on me. There is a split second, like a deer caught in the glare of an oncoming headlight, where our eyes are riveted. Then, in an instant, her knowing smile breaks the tension, and I respond in kind before she reaffixes her dark sunglasses.

On the following Thursday, the International Herald Tribune noted that earlier in the week, Sophia Loren had traveled to Rome from her home in the U.S. to receive the Italian government's highest award for cultural achievement. At the ceremony, Italy's Prime Minister, Massimo D'Alema, received a surprise kiss on the cheek from Ms. Loren on the occasion of his 50th birthday. He told her, "I'm a true admirer of yours. Thanks for the emotions you know how to give us."

The Prime Minister was graced with a kiss, but I was graced with a smile, and its place in my mind remains as bold as a Sophia Loren emotion.

GERRY LEADER'S BOOK ON LEADERSHIP

"At a time of extreme challenge for our nation's schools, *Bold School Principals* delivers extraordinary hope, in the form of rich, on-the-ground testimonies from successful school leaders. From inside the classrooms, faculty meetings, parent gatherings, and more, the book brings the unmediated stories of school principals as they do the creative, complex work of fostering teacher leadership, supporting student learning and well-being, navigating antagonistic school cultures, and empowering and protecting staff. A unique and essential roadmap for school leadership."

— Deanne Urmy, Editor-at-Large, Mariner Books

ABOUT THE AUTHOR

Gerald C. Leader (Gerry) is Professor Emeritus of Boston University. He earned an MBA in 1961 and a Doctorate in 1965 from Harvard Graduate School of Business Administration. Following his service as a commanding officer in the U.S. Army, Professor Leader's career history of five decades includes roles as an educator with leadership practice, research and teaching. He has focused on leadership, first in the private sector then in non-profit organizations, government agencies and subsequently in secondary education. In 2002, Professor Leader co-founded with Tom Scott and directed the Educator Leadership Institute (ELI), a Massachusetts state licensed principal preparation program until his retirement in 2012. He is the co-author with Amy Stern of *Real Leaders, Real Schools - Stories of Success Against Enormous Odds* published by Harvard Education Press in 2008. Professor Leader and his wife Lucy live in Brookline, Massachusetts.

Email: gleader@bu.edu

www.ingramcontent.com/pod-product-compliance
Lightning Source LLC
Chambersburg PA
CBHW050406030726
47503CB00006B/2056